How dared he suppose that she was for sale?

"You mean you'll give me the Rio contract if I go to bed with you?" Heather repeated.

"Why not?" Race shrugged negligently. "As models go, you've reached your peak. A contract like that would set you up for the rest of your life."

Heather started to shake with suppressed rage. "And if I don't agree to become your...mistress, you'll see that I don't get it."

"Clever girl," he mocked.

"But why me?"

"I want you." His eyes rested on her body. "I've wanted you from the beginning, and I'm going to have you, Heather. And you want me, too. So let's stop playing games. We both know you're going to say yes. You're too greedy to do otherwise!"

Books by Penny Jordan

HARLEQUIN PRESENTS

471—FALCON'S PREY
477—TIGER MAN
484—MARRIAGE WITHOUT LOVE
489—LONG COLD WINTER
508—NORTHERN SUNSET
517—BLACKMAIL
519—THE CAGED TIGER
537—DAUGHTER OF HASSAN
553—AN UNBROKEN MARRIAGE
562—BOUGHT WITH HIS NAME
569—ESCAPE FROM DESIRE
584—THE FLAWED MARRIAGE
591—PHANTOM MARRIAGE
602—RESCUE OPERATION
609—DESIRE'S CAPTIVE
618—A SUDDEN ENGAGEMENT
633—PASSIONATE PROTECTION
641—ISLAND OF THE DAWN
650—SAVAGE ATONEMENT
667—FORGOTTEN PASSION
706—SHADOW MARRIAGE
713—THE INWARD STORM
728—RESPONSE
738—WANTING

These books may be available at your local bookseller.

For a list of all titles currently available,
send your name and address to:

Harlequin Reader Service
P.O. Box 52040, Phoenix, AZ 85072-2040
Canadian address: P.O. Box 2800, Postal Station A,
5170 Yonge St., Willowdale, Ont. M2N 5T5

PENNY JORDAN

wanting

Harlequin Books

TORONTO • NEW YORK • LONDON
AMSTERDAM • PARIS • SYDNEY • HAMBURG
STOCKHOLM • ATHENS • TOKYO • MILAN

Harlequin Presents first edition November 1984
ISBN 0-373-10738-2

Original hardcover edition published in 1984
by Mills & Boon Limited

CHAPTER ONE

'RACE Williams is going to be there tonight—I wonder what he's like? Thirty-four is very young to be given overall control of the entire documentary section. He used to be a reporter, you know, before he started writing.'

'Does Terry know about this burgeoning hero-worship for your new boss?' Heather Martin asked her cousin dryly, surveying her petite form and clustering blonde curls.

No two girls could have been less alike. While Jennifer was petite and dainty, Heather stood five feet ten inches in her bare feet, her dark cloud of hair and long green eyes adding up to a gypsy sensuality that came across well when she was photographed. It was virtually impossible to open a magazine without seeing her own face, and she had grown used to other people's reaction to her startling good looks. She had been modelling for three years, ever since she was twenty-one, and just recently had begun to wonder what the future held. She was currently on the short list for a prestige modelling job, promoting a brand-new range of up-market cosmetics, but her real love was writing, and for the last few years she had been gathering material for her book. All she needed now was the time to write it.

'Terry says Race has asked him about you,' Jennifer announced, watching her reaction to her announcement. Terry was the art director of the television company Jennifer worked for—a new independent company which was fast gaining an excellent reputation, and which had recently 'head-hunted' Race Williams, whose reputation in the field of hard-fact documentary work was well known. He had been a Fleet Street reporter, before turning to writing 'factional' novels, and Jennifer, to judge by the amount of time she spent talking about him, seemed to be developing a crush on him.

Despite the fact that Jennifer was two years her senior, at twenty-four Heather was easily the more mature. She had lived with Jennifer, her twin brothers and her aunt and uncle since the deaths of her own parents when she was thirteen. Her father had been an explorer, her mother his researcher, and they had both been killed in an avalanche in the Andes, and Heather had never ceased to mourn their loss. Kind though her aunt and uncle were, she had always felt like a cuckoo in the nest, towering above her aunt and Jennifer, and even the twins until they suddenly started to shoot up at eighteen. Her height had always made her feel vulnerable. At school she had been the butt of cruel jokes, easily the tallest girl in the class, and she had been well on the way to developing a complex about it when she met Brad.

Brad! Her mouth tightened ominously. She had met him when she was seventeen and studying for her 'A' levels. He had just left school and started at university. He was a friend of the twins, and she hadn't been able to believe it when he started paying attention to her, asking her for dates. He was the first boy-friend she had ever had; the first boy ever to pay her the slightest attention, and under it she blossomed.

Her aunt had been delighted but concerned. Heather remembered vividly an occasion when her aunt had taken her on one side and stumbled through a muddled speech about not taking Brad too seriously. She hadn't listened. Brad loved her, he had told her so, and in her innocence and vulnerability she had thought he meant it, opening to him all the secrets of her heart and mind, content to let him dictate the pace of their relationship. She had never entered the giggled sexual discussions of her peers; she had always been an outsider, and Jennifer, in whom she might have confided, was already away at university. Brad made teasingly light love to her, and she had thought it was because he loved her that he only went so far. God, how naïve she had been!

She had found out the truth quite by accident. She and Brad had been invited to a party—a friend of Brad's, and she had gone into the kitchen looking for a drink of water. She wasn't used to alcohol, and the punch she had been given had made her acutely thirsty. She had seen Brad in the kitchen, talking to one of his friends as she approached, and was just about to greet him when she heard his friend ask, 'Who's the new girl? Hardly your type—all those muscles! What's she like in bed?'

She remembered how vividly she had coloured, embarrassed by the other boy's frankness, but nothing had prepared her for the cruelty of Brad's response.

'Who cares?' he had responded carelessly. 'Personally I prefer my women small and cuddly, but she's got a fortune coming to her on her twenty-first birthday, and I aim to make sure that by then she's my wife; I can always enjoy myself on the side.'

Heather hadn't stayed to listen to any more. It was true that she was to inherit a good deal of money from her parents' estate, but the thought that Brad deliberately intended to marry her for her money was something she found a bitter pill to accept. She hadn't said anything when he took her home; some deep-seated instinct warned her against letting him see how badly she was hurt. In fact she hadn't told anyone what she had overheard, but it had festered, aching inside her, giving her the strength to remain cool and aloof when she told Brad she didn't want to go out with him again.

He had been persistent, she gave him that, but she remained resolute, deriving a bitter satisfaction from the thought that he would never know just how much it cost her to refuse him. She had loved him; trusted him; revealed her innermost thoughts and hopes to him believing he returned her feelings. Well, she would never let it happen again.

It had been Neil, her cousin, who had suggested she take up modelling. He was a very keen photographer and his photographs had won a competition in their local paper. With the encouragement of her family Heather had approached one of the well known model agencies, who had agreed with Neil's judgment. Only to herself was Heather prepared to admit that her fierce determination to succeed had sprung from the pain she experienced when Brad derided her. She was consumed by a need to prove to him and the world at large that she *was* desirable, and she *had* proved it.

She smiled without mirth, thinking of the number of proposals and propositions she had received in the last three years, but none of them had touched her. They weren't from men who loved her, who cared genuinely and deeply about her, all they had been interested in was the satisfaction of their own desire. Oh, they might wrap it up in pretty words and compliments, but Heather knew better. And now here was Jennifer telling her that Race Williams had been making enquiries about her.

She wasn't totally surprised. As a model she was used to the interest she aroused in men. Only she knew that inside the cool detachment she showed to the outside world she was still the same vulnerable, hurting girl who had stood in the shadows and listened to the person she loved destroying her world.

'What did Race Williams want to know about me?' she asked her cousin. They were both eating their evening meal. Heather didn't need to diet to keep her lissom shape, and she drank her coffee, grateful for its fragrant warmth as Jennifer studied her.

'Oh, the usual things,' she grinned, 'were you attached, etc., etc. Terry must have told him you were my cousin. . . .' She saw the look on Heather's face and warned anxiously, 'Heather, he isn't one of your usual men, you can't play the same games with him you do with them.'

'Games?' Heather raised one immaculate eyebrow.

'Come off it, you know what I mean,' Jennifer interrupted crossly. 'Look, honey, I've seen you in action; the come-on and then the put-down; the whole bit. There hasn't been a man in your life since Brad who's even come close to touching your emotions, but with every one you let them think you've fallen—hard—and then you pull the rug out from under.'

Heather frowned at this accurate and rather unattractive picture her cousin drew. 'Oh, look, I'm not criticising,' Jennifer assured her, 'far from it, I'm just saying that Race Williams isn't like all the others. He's hard, Heather, and he won't let you get away with it, so if that's what you're planning on doing, don't, please.'

'I wasn't planning on doing anything,' Heather assured her cousin. It was true, Heather always let the men do the running, and not until she was sure they deserved it did she let them see her contempt for them. They were all the same; all so egotistically sure of themselves and her ultimate surrender to them that they deserved the treatment she handed out.

'When do you get to hear about the Rio contract?' Jennifer asked her, changing the subject.

'Oh, I think they're making the final decision within the next few days. Four of us are shortlisted, and I'm the only brunette.'

'They're bound to choose you,' Jennifer assured her warmly. 'You're so right for the image they want to promote.'

Privately Heather agreed, and she had already made up her mind that if she got this contract it would be her last. She would retire and concentrate on her book. She knew there had been a considerable degree of speculation in the fashion press about the contract and she was hotly tipped as favourite.

'Come on, time to get ready,' announced Jennifer, getting up. The party was to celebrate the television company's first year in business and the appointment of Race Williams. Jennifer's invitation had extended to cover a friend and Heather had agreed to go with her. One of the shareholders in the TV company was also a shareholder in Rio, and a little public relations work wouldn't come amiss. Not that Heather ever used either her beauty or her body to further her career. It was the inviolateness of her body and mind that gave her the power to destroy the male sex; her strength came from the fact that secretly she despised them. She was glad Brad had left her a virgin, she thought fiercely, and she intended to stay that way, giving nothing of herself to any man, because giving meant receiving pain in return; and she'd had enough of that.

In her room she abandoned her thoughts and studied her reflection with professional scrutiny. Her face was heart-shaped, her eyes set wide apart, deeply green and tilted at the corners, her mouth warmly curved, her cloud of dark hair reaching down on to her shoulders. Hers was a sensual face, one which was used to market goods with a high degree of sexual appeal, but inwardly Heather felt her nature was completely at odds with her looks. Inwardly she was as cold and devoid of sensuality as a lump of ice, and it was this that made it so easy for her to revenge herself on the male sex; they took one look at her face and her tall languidly curved body and mentally docketed her as 'easy'. She laughed mirthlessly. Nothing could have been further from the truth, and in time, with varying degrees of humiliation, they all discovered it. She had perfected a form of put-down that sliced into the delicate male ego like a knife through butter, and every time the look in their eyes was the same. But best of all, they never warned the next victim; never admitted their humiliation, leaving her free to repeat the whole process over and over again. She smiled when she read the names of her supposed 'lovers' in the press, smiled in genuine amusement, her reputation protected her from men who might have found her virginity a challenge they would commit rape to overcome, and that was the way she liked it.

Her dress for the evening was in fine black matt jersey; striking décolleté, sweeping down to her waist at the front revealing the smooth cream flesh of her rounded breasts and the narrow vulnerability of her rib cage. At the back it exposed her body right down to the base of her spine and it fitted her like another layer of skin. An advantage of her height was that she was able to carry off the ripe fullness of her breasts without seeming badly proportioned, their curves in direct contrast to the narrowness of her hips and the slender length of her legs. Black silk panties were the only thing she wore under her dress. Her legs were still slightly tanned from her last modelling trip abroad, her toenails painted a deeply vibrant pink.

So Race Williams had been asking about her ... Heather quickly collated all that she knew about him. They had never met, she had no idea what he looked like, but the gossip columnists loved him; he had featured as an escort of many beautiful women, and he had a reputation for ending his affairs when they began to bore him that made her eyes gleam and harden with the anticipation of battle. It would be very pleasant to humiliate a man like that; a man who treated her sex so contemptuously. Perhaps he was already contemplating making her his latest conquest. The thought wasn't formed through vanity—what man would want the girl she had been, the vulnerable woman she still was inside? Oh no, she didn't delude herself on that issue. What Race Williams and men like him wanted was the outer shell she presented to the world; the looks that adorned the covers of magazines; the kudos of escorting a newsworthy female; or possessing her and subjugating her to their male power.

'Heather, are you ready yet?' she heard Jennifer call outside her door. 'The taxi will be here soon!'

Quickly completing her make-up, Heather brushed her hair, watching it billow on to her bare shoulders, recognising the glitter in her eyes and the colour gleaming on her cheekbones, and knowing the reason for them.

'Thank God Terry likes small blondes,' Jennifer pronounced piously as Heather opened the door. 'My God, you're really going to town tonight!' She watched as Heather slipped on high-heeled sandals, wondering how tall Race Williams was. In her high heels she topped six foot, and it always amused her to witness a man's initial reaction to that fact. Some, she knew, found her height sexually exciting, visualising her as some sort of Amazon in bed, and initially she was careful not to disillusion them.

'You'll need your fur jacket,' Jennifer told her, 'the temperature was starting to drop when I came in. I hate January and February,' she added, shuddering, 'and we're only just into January—brrr!'

Laughing, Heather reached inside her wardrobe for her jacket. Both girls had been presented with them as Christmas presents that year. Jennifer's was a soft silky blue fox which suited her fair colouring, and Heather's a richly dark silver fox, in which her uncle had told her fondly that she looked magnificent. Dear Uncle Bob; he and the twins were the only men she actually liked and felt at ease with. The twins were as close to her as brothers and her aunt and uncle had taken the place of her deceased parents, but still there was this sense of loss, of not truly belonging, of always, somehow, being on the outside. Which was why she had responded so passionately to Brad's attentions; needing the commitment of sharing her feeling with someone else; needing to feel 'special' to another person. She sighed, pushing away all thoughts of the past, following Jennifer outside.

The television studio was several miles from their flat and they arrived to find it well lit, the car-park full of expensive, prestige pieces of metal. Male toys needed to boost fragile male egos.

The commissionaire recognised Jennifer and welcomed her with a grin, but it was on Heather that his eyes lingered admiringly.

'Another conquest,' Jennifer murmured as they got in the lift. 'Oh, don't look like that—I'm not a fool, Heather,' she told her cousin. 'I know you don't give a damn for any of those men you go out with. I also know that when you're supposed to be having mad flings with them, you're tucked up safely in your own virginal bed.' She saw Heather's expression and said quietly, 'It's true, isn't it?' Without waiting for an answer she went on, 'I'm not going to pry, but Heather, you're heading for trouble, honey. One day a man's going to come along who you can't play with, and he's going to think it's all for real. By the time he finds out the truth, it's going to be too late. You know what I'm trying to say, don't you?'

'Yes, and you needn't worry. I'm immune to sexual come-ons, Jen; frigid, if you prefer me to use that term.'

'Frigid? Or frightened?' Jennifer asked acutely as they stepped out of the lift. 'I'm two years older than you, cos, and I can remember quite vividly how shy and sensitive you were in your teens. That girl hasn't completely disappeared. I know you, you're already plotting the downfall of the next poor victim, but take care the roles aren't reversed—if you're thinking in terms of Race Williams, remember he eats women for breakfast!'

'And changes them as frequently as he changes his pure silk shirts—yes, I know, but I never make the running, Jen. If Race Williams wants me he's going to have to let me know it.'

'And once he does you're going to put him down, humiliate him like you've done the others. Heather, I've watched you. Oh, you've got away with it because none of them want to admit the truth, but Race Williams isn't like that. He's tough, and he's got a temper. He doesn't play the game by the rules, and with him civilisation is just a veneer.'

'You seem to know a lot about him,' commented Heather.

'I've heard the rumours, Terry knows him quite well. They were at Oxford together, apparently.'

'Bully for Terry,' Heather muttered in a voice that made her cousin raise her eyebrows, although she refrained from saying anything because the lift doors had opened and half a dozen people were already milling around in the small space outside.

'We'll leave our jackets in my office,' Jennifer told her. 'The cloakroom's only small and it will be crowded.' Jennifer's office was a bare room at the end of a long corridor, and Heather was familiar with it from previous visits. She took off her jacket, hanging it in the small cupboard, waiting patiently while Jennifer checked her make-up without even looking at her own.

'Okay, that's it,' Jennifer announced when she had finished applying her lipstick. 'I warned Terry to save us a table and I told him what time we were arriving, so with a bit of luck he should have got us drinks.'

Heather knew Terry Brady quite well. Jennifer had flitted from man to man like a bee in search of honey until she met Terry, with whom she swore she had fallen in love at first sight. At the moment she wasn't sure whether he returned her feelings, but she was determined to give him every opportunity to find out.

The moment they entered the crowded studio which was being used for the party Heather spotted Terry. He was sitting at a table with another man, his fair head turned towards him. As though he knew they were there his companion lifted his head and looked towards them, his eyes riveted on Heather's face. For some reason she was consumed by a wave of heat, burning slowly up her body, leaving her feeling as though she had been completely robbed of energy. Although he was too far away for her to study properly, Heather had a vivid impression of darkly male features; a face stamped with arrogance and masculinity, dark hair growing low over a white shirt collar, lean brown hands and the shocking and inescapable feeling that he had just slowly and thoroughly removed her clothes and then caressed every inch of the skin he had revealed.

'Can you see Terry?' Jennifer asked her, standing on tiptoe.

'No, but I have seen someone I want to talk to, an old friend,' she fibbed. 'Look, why don't you go and look for Terry, and then I'll come and find you later.'

Jennifer squirmed uncomfortably. 'I wish you'd come with me,' she protested, adding hurriedly, 'Well, Race asked Terry if you were coming, and he suggested we make up a foursome. They'll be waiting for us, and. . . .'

'I thought you'd just warned me against him?' Heather reminded her cousin wryly.

'Against trying to make a fool of him,' Jennifer shot back. 'Look, he only wants to meet you. . . .'

'To meet me, presumably as a prelude to bedding me,' Heather agreed bluntly. 'Look, I'm sorry if it embarrasses you, but I'm not going to be manipulated. I'll join you later when I've spoken to Donna.'

So Race Williams wanted to meet her, did he? Her heart contracted on a fierce wave of anger as she remembered the look Terry's companion had given her. He had to be Race Williams, she was sure of it, and equally sure that there was no way she was going to be manoeuvred into spending the evening with him. If he wanted her, then let him find out the hard way, as others had done before him, that he was going to have to work hard at trying to get her. And he did want her—she had seen it in the look he gave her. It had been ferociously sexual, and not simply sexual, there had been a hint of possession which sent fear coiling along her spine, even while she shrugged it aside. Heavens, there was nothing to be afraid of, he represented nothing she couldn't handle, just as she had handled men like him before.

Eventually Jennifer left, plainly none too happy

about doing so, and Heather was free to walk in the direction of the bar. She was stopped half a dozen times by people who recognised her, all of them male, and she parried their questions and compliments with her cool, languorous smile, never realising that the languor beneath the ice was what fired their blood, and excited their masculinity.

From the vantage point of her height she was able to see Terry's table relatively clearly, although she took good care to study it discreetly. Race Williams had his back to her. She watched him stand up as Jennifer approached, Terry frowning slightly and then glancing around the room.

Poor Terry—she hoped her non-appearance wouldn't count as a black mark against him. She had already decided that she was going to leave just as soon as she could order a taxi, unwilling as yet to analyse the instinct for flight rather than fight.

As she watched Heather saw Race Williams get up and disappear, presumably going to the bar, and she let out the breath she hadn't realised she was holding. Now was her opportunity to make her escape. Escape? She was being rather dramatic, wasn't she?

She found the corridor leading to Jennifer's office without too much difficulty, not bothering to switch on the light as she walked inside. She was just reaching for her jacket when the hairs on the back of her neck prickled warningly and she swung round, her heart thudding as she found herself confronted by the very man she wanted to avoid.

He was taller than she had imagined, six four at least, arms folded across his chest, his lean body completely at ease as he rested against the door, blocking her exit.

'Leaving already?' he drawled.

'I have a headache,' she smiled, keeping her voice

even and pleasant. 'I'm sorry,' she added, deliberately casual, 'I don't believe we've met. . . .'

He snapped on the light, almost blinding her with its brilliance, his mouth creasing into a humourless smile as he drawled mockingly, 'Nice try, Heather, but it won't work. You know who I am, just as I know who you are. Terry's told me a good deal about you.'

'Terry?'

'Umm, I asked him. You see, I've been wanting to meet you for quite a long time. You're a very beautiful woman,' he added softly, 'and extremely desirable. . . . I'd very much like to go to bed with you.'

Heather hid the anger she could feel boiling up inside her.

'But then you already know that, don't you?' Race Williams continued in a smokily seductive voice. 'You knew that the moment you saw me tonight. What I don't understand is why that knowledge made you run away from me. Because you are running, aren't you?' He laughed softly when she didn't answer. 'You're giving me a psychological advantage, Heather. Why are you frightened of me?'

'I'm not,' Heather retorted coolly, gathering her scattered wits, 'and neither am I running.'

'Then come back to the studio and dance with me. Something tells me we'd move very well together, you and I.'

She forced herself not to acknowledge the sexual undertones of his comment.

'I hear you're in the running for the Rio contract,' he commented, suddenly changing the subject, relaxing the sexual pressure, she recognised suspiciously, wondering at the change in tactics. 'Do you want the contract?'

She raised her eyebrows. 'Of course. If I didn't I wouldn't be in the running, as you put it, would I?'

'And you're hot favourite to get it. I can see why, but the competition is pretty tough. I hear you're also a writer.'

Heather's eyes hardened. Damn Jennifer and her careless tongue! She hated anyone knowing about her writing. The family knew, of course, but that was all. She had been a dreamy adolescent when she first knew she wanted to write, and the urge had never left her.

'I'm interested in lots of things,' was her careful answer, but she wished she hadn't given it, when he agreed laconically.

'My sex being one of them, so I hear. You go through men like other women go through pairs of tights.'

'Perhaps I'm choosy.'

'Then choose me.' Suddenly he had closed the distance between them, and she was intimately aware of the heat coming off his body, the desire glittering in the dark grey eyes as they roamed restlessly over her. Fear knifed through her, a sharp throat-gagging fear she had never experienced before and which held her motionless as his hands slid down her shoulders, exploring the shape and texture of her back, forcing her against the unwanted intimacy of his body, making her burningly aware of the power and maleness of him, her mind fastidiously outraged by the pulsating hardness of his body when his hands gripped her hips. She shouldn't have come here, she should have made sure he hadn't seen her leave the studio. Here they were alone and there was no way she could fight him.

'I want you, Heather.' Race Williams kept on saying it as though saying the words reinforced his belief that he had every right to take what he wanted. Heather could feel her body tensing, recoiling from his, fear coiling through her stomach, acrid on her tongue. He bent his head and she knew he was going to kiss her.

She forced her body to relax, wrenching herself out of his arms as he relaxed his grip, and snatching up her coat, turned for the door.

'Well, I don't want you!' she told him furiously, cool disparagement forgotten as rage flicked through her veins. How dared he assume that she was his simply for the taking, that he could state his desire and blandly assume she would assuage it! 'Men like you make me sick,' she told him in a low voice, the pent-up loathing of years thickening it until it was only a husky whisper, her eyes emerald in her pale face. 'If you want a toy to play with, go buy yourself a Barbie doll! I'm fussy about the men who share my life.'

'That wasn't the way I heard it.' They faced one another like two antagonists. Heather could see the rage simmering in the molten heat of his eyes sharpened by sexual frustration, the intensity of his emotions half frightening her as she watched him, wary as any animal scenting the hunter.

'I want you,' he repeated thickly, 'and I damn well mean to have you. . . .'

'Never!' The denial was out before she could silence it, lying between them like a gage, anger and frustration mingling in his expression, his chest rising and falling as though he had been running. Without pausing to think Heather turned, running down the corridor and out into the foyer, pressing the button for the lift. Jennifer would wonder what had happened to her, but she would just have to wonder. She glanced over her shoulder half expecting to find that Race had followed her, but there was no sign of him. He was probably still trying to come to terms with the blow she had just dealt his mammoth self-esteem.

She could hardly believe he was real, she thought, mentally re-living their conversation. Had he actually thought all he had to do was say he wanted her for her to fall into his arms? Was that what normally happened? There was a raw maleness about him that some women might find appealing, an overt sexuality that she found totally repelling, frightening almost, but that other women might enjoy. His arrogant assumption that she was his simply for the asking still had the power to stun her. She had met some self-assured men in her time, but they had nothing on him. No wonder Jennifer had warned her against him!

Well, she needn't worry, Heather thought grimly as she got out of the lift and asked the commissionaire to get her a taxi. There was simply no way she was ever going to get within a mile of Race Williams knowingly again.

He had frightened her—she could admit that from the sanctuary of her taxi. His determination had overwhelmed her, threatening all her carefully erected barriers. He wasn't a man she could lead on and then drop, he wouldn't stand by and let her dismiss him.

She was in bed but awake when Jennifer came in, and called out to her. Jennifer looked defensive and slightly guilty when she walked in.

'I'm sorry,' she apologised without Heather having to speak, 'but he made Terry promise to introduce you to him. He was furious when I turned up without you. He went looking for you.'

'And found me,' Heather told her grimly. 'It's high time someone taught Mr Race Williams that he can't get everything he wants simply by demanding it. Relax,' she added when she saw Jennifer's face, 'I value my skin far too much to try it.'

'He wants you, Heather,' Jennifer told her uneasily, 'and he won't let go. He kept on asking me about you. It was frightening . . . he's almost obsessive about you. Perhaps you ought to go out with him, let him see what you're really like—behind the model-girl mask.

He likes sophisticated worldly women, when he realises what you're really like. . . .'

'I don't want to hear another word about him,' Heather told her, pulling the bedclothes over her head. 'Not another word.'

CHAPTER TWO

THE phone rang and Heather jumped, eyeing it dubiously. She had been tense all day, and all because of Race Williams. The desire she had seen flaming in his eyes had unnerved her. She wasn't a stranger to men's desire, she reminded herself, and he wasn't the first man to make it plain to her in a first meeting that he wanted her, it happened all the time, but there was something different about him; an intensity and determination that alarmed her.

She picked up the receiver at the fourth ring, relieved to hear her agent's voice on the other end. 'Good news, I think,' he told her, 'You've been summoned for another interview for the Rio contract. One of the directors this time. I'll give you the address. They want you there at three o'clock sharp. I haven't heard of any of the others being sent for, so I'll keep my fingers crossed for you.'

Heather replaced the receiver and glanced into the hall mirror. Her reflection looked unfamiliar, her eyes dark and clouded, her mouth tremulously full, intensifying the sensual attraction of her features. She knew she ought to be feeling glad about the interview, but instead she merely felt restless, impatient with the constant round of interviews; of move and counter-move, and she yearned to be free to be herself, not a marketable commodity.

Nevertheless she went into her room and carefully selected the outfit she would wear for the interview. The Rio cosmetics range was essentially glamour cosmetics and that was the image she would have to

23

project. She chose a black suit, the skirt fitted and fairly short. The jacket was tailored to follow the lines of her body, flaring out gently just below the waist, the sleeves slightly full. With it she wore a white silk blouse, and Dior stockings. She swept her hair up into a chignon and sat down to put on her hat, carefully arranging its spotted net veil. The finished effect was one of carefully contrived sophistication underlining her sensuality. Jennifer, who had the day off, came in loaded down with shopping just as she went into the living room. 'Wow', she exclaimed with a grin. 'What's the big occasion.'

Heather told her.

'Umm, well you should get top marks for that outfit, especially if it's a man. It simply shrieks sexy underwear,' she added obliquely, but Heather knew what she meant, and said dryly that that was the whole idea.

The address she had been given was in Mayfair, and she managed to find a taxi to take her there without too much difficulty. A manservant opened the door to her ring, showing her into some sort of waiting room, its furnishings as uninspiring as those in any busy doctor's surgery. In the distance Heather could hear someone typing, and she sat down, trying to empty her mind and concentrate on the interview ahead. There had been half a dozen of them already. Rio was a new concept and the directors seemed unable to agree on exactly what image they wished to project. Ten and then fifteen minutes ticked by, and her thoughts strayed back to the previous evening. She could feel the tension and anger rising inside her as she remembered the way Race Williams had looked and talked. She had met men like him before, she reminded herself, men who thought women existed solely for their pleasure; and she detested them. This man was not so different, merely more dangerously sensual; more explicit in his intentions. She quelled a briefly impulsive desire to puncture his conceit, to destroy the monstrous ego that made him think his attentions might be welcomed.

What kind of a woman did he think she was? She grimaced. She already knew the answer to that one, and curiously enough resented the reasoning behind it with an intensity that startled her. She glanced at her watch and tapped her foot impatiently. Why was she being kept waiting like this? She got up and opened the door, the hall was empty, the sound of typing louder. Frowning Heather listened to it. Perhaps they had forgotten about her?

Without giving herself time too think she marched towards the door behind which she could hear the typewriter and knocked, her eyes widening in stunned shock as she saw the man sitting behind the large desk.

'I'm sorry Heather,' he apologised blandly. 'Did you think I'd forgotten about you?'

'You!' It was all Heather could manage to say. What was Race Williams doing here? 'What are you doing here?' she demanded baldly, 'I've. . . .'

'You've come to see one of the directors of Rio, he interrupted smoothly, 'Quite right. That's me.' He rose from the desk and came to stand in front of it, leaning back, arms folded as he studied her. 'Very nice,' he added when he had finished. 'Not quite as provocative as what you were wearing last night. You must wear that dress for me again Heather,' he added softly. 'What there was of it made me ache to take it off you.' His eyes rested on her breasts and to Heather's furious confusion she felt their involuntary response and knew without having to look down; without hearing his soft, satisfied laugh, that her nipples were tautly outlined against the thin fabric of her suit.

'You tricked me into coming here,' Heather ground out, turning back to the door, 'I. . . .'

'Not really,' he said smoothly. 'I *am* a director of Rio with enough shares to make sure you get the contract, if. . . .'

'If?' She turned to stare at him, hardly able to believe she was not imagining that delicate pause; hardly able to accept that he was actually going to say what she suspected.

'I've done a little more research on you since last night, Heather,' he told her softly. 'And from what I've learned it seems plain that you and I got off on the wrong foot. Now, if I were to promise you that you would get the modelling contract for Rio, I'm sure. . . .'

'It would persuade me to go to bed with you?' Heather inserted, hardly knowing how she kept from screaming the words at him.

'Oh I wouldn't put it as crudely as that. Let's just say I'm sure you're nothing like as hard as your detractors suggest, and that pure kind-heartedness would persuade you to assuage my . . . desire?'

Dear God, she didn't believe this. 'You mean you'll give me the Rio contract if I go to bed with you?' she said bluntly. 'For how long?'

'For as long as it takes,' he said gently. For as long as it took for him to grow tired of her he must mean. She started to shake with repressed rage. How dare he insult her like this; how dare he suppose even for one moment that she was for sale?

'And if I agree?' Some biting urge to discover just how avaricious he actually thought she was prompted her to go on. 'What proof do I have that. . . .'

He looked at the phone. 'I'll arrange it whilst you're here, provided you make a small down payment as proof of sincerity first,' he added mildly.

'I can't believe you mean this,' she said the words to herself more than to him but he heard her and his face tightened.

'Oh, believe me, I do,' he said softly. 'You ran from me last night Heather, you made it plain just how much you loathed the thought of me. You rejected me—publicly. Publicly . . .' he continued when she would have interrupted, 'Terry knows . . . Jennifer knows. I'm not a man who likes being humiliated.'

If that was the case he shouldn't have assumed that she would simply fall into his arms, Heather thought feverishly.

'You need that contract,' he told her. 'As models go, you've reached your peak. This contract will set you up nicely for the rest of your life.' He obviously didn't know that she had money of her own, Heather decided; and that she could easily afford to fling his threats back in his face.

'And if I don't agree to become your . . . mistress, you'll make sure I don't get the contract.'

'Clever girl,' he mocked.

'But why me?'

'Why not me?' he encountered. 'What have all the other men in your life had that I don't?'

If she told him he'd never believe her, Heather thought watching him silently menacing her, waiting for her to fall into his trap.

'Come on Heather,' he said grimly, suddenly very much at the end of his patience. 'What difference can one more man make, and think of the benefits?'

'I'm surprised you're prepared to go to such lengths,' she said dryly, trying to buy time to think. 'I shouldn't have thought a man like you would need *to* go to them to get female companionship.'

'I don't, normally, and I doubt I would now, if it wasn't for the fact that I don't like being made a fool of,' he told her, his face hardening. 'Everyone saw the way you avoided me last night; and half of them knew I'd deliberately set things up so that I could meet you . . . and like I said,' his eyes rested on her body. 'I want you.'

Well, you're not having me. The words were on the tip of Heather's tongue, but she suppressed them. No. She'd played along with him for a while; let him think he'd won her and then. . . . A tiny inner voice warned her that she was playing with fire, but she ignored it.

'So it would seem,' she agreed, dropping her voice to a soft purr.

'And I'll make *you* want *me*,' he told her.

Did he honestly think he could? She almost laughed aloud. Here at least she was safe. 'You think so?'

'I know so.'

His arrogance almost robbed her of breath.

'Come on, Heather, let's stop playing games. I know the sort of woman you are, and your type doesn't normally appeal to me, but there's something about you, and it's got right under my skin. You make me itch to possess you,' he told her frankly.

'I wonder what your co-directors would say if they knew about the offer you've made me?' she murmured coolly.

He laughed. 'If you're threatening to tell them, I shouldn't bother. You see, Heather, they've already made their choice and it isn't you, but as I'm the major shareholder I can make them change that choice. If you go running to them, all they'll do is assume it's sour grapes.'

Was he telling the truth? What did it matter? She would have liked the contract but not to the extent that she was willing to barter herself for it.

'Could I have some time to think about it?' she asked, watching him.

He laughed and shook his head. 'I promised myself that you'd share my bed last night, Heather, and I don't take easily to frustration. I want your answer now; and your commitment. But we both know you're going to say "yes", don't we?' he said easily, infuriating her still further. 'You're too greedy to refuse.'

Battening down her anger, Heather looked at him, and then said carefully and clearly, 'For the last time, there is nothing, no inducement you could offer, that would make me share your bed. Your ego is enormous; your arrogance unbelievable.' She saw the colour sting along the high cheekbones and continued remorselessly. 'I don't need the Rio contract; and even if I did I'd refuse it. You dare to try and blackmail me into bed with you? What kind of man are you. . . .'

'I'll show you, shall I?' he ground out, reaching for her, so quickly that she was caught off guard, his fingers snapping round her wrists, imprisoning her, the strength of their tensile grip too much for her to resist. Suddenly she felt extremely vulnerable, and Heather knew with shocked insight that she had pushed him too far. As he held her she knew exactly what it was to experience fear. For a moment her anger had been so great that she simply hadn't thought. Despite her height there was simply no way she could free herself from the grip of his hands, and panic, wild, and disordered shot through her, making her struggle frantically, poise and cool control forgotten as she felt the heat coming off his body and knew her struggles were arousing him.

When his body touched hers she shrank from it, shocked by the sensations coursing through her; totally alien and yet in some way, intensely familiar, as though some part of her had always known they were there but had rigorously held them at bay. As she looked up into Race's eyes she saw his expression change, sharpening, watching; whilst her body started to tremble in primitive response to his touch. She didn't understand what was happening to her. He was everything she loathed and detested, and yet . . .

His hands slid from her waist to her back finding and stroking along her spine. She tried to remind herself that Race was simply trying to punish her, but her body refused to listen. The moment he touched her it had been like the beginning of a nightmare; all her defences swept away, not by him, but by her reaction to him. She still hated and loathed everything that he was but he was right; inexplicably, horrifyingly, she wanted him! The knowledge was enough to make her freeze in his arms, hoping that his anger had died down enough for her to reason with him.

'Heather.'

She heard her name and looked up, gasping as his hands slipped up to her shoulders holding her against his body, his mouth searingly hot against hers, his tongue probing the tense outline of her lips. Her head was swimming with the rage of need suddenly out of control inside her. No man had ever made her feel like this; she didn't even like him, she kept repeating soundlessly, but her body wasn't listening. Race had already found the buttons on her shirt, his fingers impatient as he tugged them open, her startled murmur giving him the access he wanted to the moist interior of her mouth. She tried to fight against the insidious pull of the desire she could feel building up inside her, forcing herself to remember why she had come here, but it was as though all her barriers had suddenly come down, as though Race's touch was the magic key to turn the locks she had always secured against his sex.

And she wasn't alone in her desire. What had started out as anger had changed swiftly—for both of them. In the heat of his body against hers, she could feel his arousal; see it in the glitter of the eyes that searched her face, his mouth wry as he pulled away to mutter thickly, 'My God, I don't believe this. One moment I want to wring your neck, the next all I can think about is having you in my bed, feeling you burn up against me, wanting me in the same way I want you. And you do want me, don't you, my lovely Heather?'

Perhaps if he hadn't bent his head to touch her throat with his lips, his hand stroking sensuously against the curve of her breast she might have found the strength to deny him. What she was doing was wrong; every instinct she possessed told her that—every instinct bar one, and that one clamoured above all the rest for satisfaction. Her body, starved of all that he was offering it for so long, blindly over-rode the danger signals from her brain. When Race left her to close the curtains she simply stood there, swaying slightly, her gaze fixed on the log fire burning in the grate, her body knowing without her having to look, the exact moment when he came to stand behind her, gently removing her jacket and hat, his hands on her shoulders turning her to him, a smile darkening his eyes as he murmured, 'I think I prefer the outfit you had on last night——'

She opened her mouth, and he laid his fingers across it. 'No, don't say anything. Last night when I saw you I thought you were the most exciting thing I'd seen in years. I wanted you so badly I could have taken you there and then—like an adolescent,' he told her with a grimace, 'and then you ran.' His eyes smouldered darkly over her face. 'No woman runs away from me, Heather—no woman makes a fool of

me the way you did. I want you. And you want me
too,' he told her, 'I know you do.'

That was the trouble, Heather thought weakly,
closing her eyes as his hands reached for her blouse,
she did. So badly that she was shaking with it, unable
to marshal any coherent or logical thoughts, her whole
being concentrated on the man in front of her and the
ache gradually spreading through her body.

She let him remove her blouse, shuddering strongly
when he peeled it back to reveal the pale flesh of her
breasts, inadequately concealed in the lace bra she was
wearing. She felt him tugging down the zip on her
skirt but even when it joined the rest of her clothes on
the floor she felt incapable of protest. She felt his
hands tremble as he reached for the fastening of her
bra, and as his hands moved slowly upwards, cupping
her aroused breasts, anguish and desire mingled
inside her, her eyes closing involuntarily as Race
bent his head, his mouth burning her skin, her body
on fire from his touch, shaking in his arms as he pulled
her tautly against his hips, letting her feel the extent of
his arousal.

'You're burning me up inside, Heather,' he
muttered hoarsely against her skin. 'Feel.' Somehow
his shirt had come unfastened, and his skin was
damply hot beneath her palms, her body arching
instinctively against the rhythmic thrust of his. He was
taking her too far, too fast, warning bells jangled in
her brain, the intensity of her own response, confusing
her, deafening her to the urgings of her mind, her
body fused against him by the heat of their mutual
need. She could feel him tremble as his mouth
explored the column of her throat, his teeth nipping
the delicate flesh.

Common sense intruded for a moment as she turned
her head and saw the totally absorbed and intensely

aroused expression on his face, fear streaking through her. What was she doing letting this man make love to her? She didn't know him; she didn't like him. She tried to pull away but his hands slid to her hips, holding her, the darkness of his head against her breast unleashing a wild tide of sensation that obliterated everything else. When he picked her up and carried her over to the leather chesterfield by the fire, she made no demur. For a long time he simply stared down at her, slowly examining every inch of her flesh until her body seemed to burn beneath the heat of his exploration. His hand caressed her thigh making her clench her hands and writhe in pleasure against him, her eyes flying open as he muttered something urgently, removing his jeans and coming to lie beside her, the heat and power of his body overwhelming her for a second so that she tensed in fear until she felt the seductive warmth of his tongue against her nipples, the suddenly harsh and changed tenor of his breathing, telling her that the caress gave him as much pleasure as it did her. The instinctive arching of her body against him, her nails raking urgently against his skin, made him groan and reach for her hips.

'I'm burning up for you, Heather,' he muttered unsteadily against her skin. 'You're a witch, do you know that? I can't remember when a woman last made me feel like this. Make love to me,' he pleaded huskily. 'Dear God, you can't know how much I need to feel your hands and mouth on my body. Last night when I got home I couldn't sleep for thinking about you; wanting you.'

He moved against her and Heather could feel the rhythmic urgency within him. Her own body seemed to surge in response, melting against him, her teeth biting into his shoulder, as his hands swept up her body and she was enveloped in fierce sheets of desire, her senses filled by the sight, smell and sound of him, wanting his possession.

She felt him move purposefully against her, the hard hunger of his body an urgent need, her gasp of pleasure as he licked her nipples making him mutter thickly into her skin. 'I can't wait much longer, Heather,' he warned her, and the sound of his voice brought her wrenchingly back to her senses, fear, and the appalled, bitter realisation of what she was doing tearing through her. She jerked away instinctively, aware of his tensed disbelief and the frustrated rage emanating from him.

'Something on account,' she reminded him, hardly recognising her own voice, 'that was all. . . .'

She heard him swear and flinched beneath the explicitness of the words he used. Pulling on her clothes, her breathing ragged, her every instinct urged her to get away, to escape before it was too late, only one tiny inner voice protesting that it was already too late, much, much too late.

She reached the door before he could stop her, nearly bumping into the manservant who had let her in, in the hall. What on earth must he think, or was he used to half-dressed women coming out of his employer's office? Had Race used the same ploy with others as he had on her?

The thought made her feel acutely sick. How could she have allowed him to touch her as he had? What on earth had happened to her. She loathed men like him; she hated any man touching her and yet in his arms she had . . . responded like an intensely passionate woman. She forced herself to admit it as her trembling legs carried her out in to the street.

There was probably a rational explanation. Her reaction could have been fuelled by her anger; anger was a primitive and intense emotion. Race was a skilled lover; it was her body that responded, not her mind, she told herself, but it was not particularly comforting. Neither her body nor her mind had ever responded like that before.

The first thing she did when she reached her flat was to pick up the phone and tell her agent that she wanted to pull out of the Rio contract. He tried to argue her out of it, but she remained steadfast.

'I want you to ring them and tell them now,' she told him, refusing to give any explanation for her decision. Once she had finished her call, she paced the flat, tense as a caged animal. She had to get away, to escape before Race found some other way of hunting her down and trapping her. She feared him. She acknowledged it now, and not simply because he wanted her. She feared her own reaction to him, the primitive desire for possession she sensed within him. She wasn't short of money. She could go abroad . . . concentrate on her writing.

Yes, that's what she would do, she decided feverishly. She would give up modelling for good . . . she could afford to. She was still pacing the floor when Jennifer came in. She took one look at her strained face and rushed over to her in concern.

'What happened?' she demanded.

'Race Williams,' Heather told her grimly. 'No . . . I don't want to talk about it. Jen, I've got to get away,' she told her cousin. 'He frightens me. . . .'

'You should be flattered that he's showing such an interest in you,' Jennifer told her. 'You know, at first I thought he simply wanted to add you to his list of conquests, but now I'm not so sure. I think he's really fallen for you, Heather.'

Her cousin's incuarbly romantic nature made Heather groan. there had been no love in the way Race had touched her body; no tender adoration, only angry male need, and she, God help her, had responded to it, had been set on fire by it; the ultimate betrayal, but he would never know that he was the only man who had made her feel like that.

'Why don't you give him a chance?' Jennifer urged. 'You both got off on the wrong foot. He's crazy about you, Heather. Terry says he was furious when you ducked out of the foursome the other night. I hadn't realised he was so involved, but Terry told me that even before he knew we were cousins or that Terry knew you, he was interested in you. . . .'

Through her involvement in the Rio contract, Heather surmised, guessing that she was correct when Jennifer asked ingenuously, 'He's even got some magazine pictures of you in his desk. One of the secretaries saw them. I'm sure he's fallen for you. Just give him a chance! Okay, he frightened you with the sexy come-on, but he doesn't know that. . . .'

'I'm still a virgin?' Heather supplied grimly. 'No, and I don't want him to know. Promise me you won't say a word about it? Promise me, Jen?'

'Of course I won't,' her cousin assured her softly. 'What do you think I am? But sooner or later you're going to have to tell him,' she said mischievously, 'or he'll find out for himself. You can't keep him at bay for ever! Come on, admit it,' she coaxed, 'you aren't entirely indifferent to him. You couldn't be, no woman could.'

'Perhaps I'm not,' Heather agreed, 'but I've no intention of becoming just another bow on his string of women.'

'I'm sure if you just give him a chance you'll find out he really cares about you,' Jennifer assured her.

Heather said nothing, not even pointing out that her cousin had changed her tune. She felt drained of all emotion other than a primeval sense of fear. Race haunted her; every time she closed her eyes she saw his face, saw the passion in it and felt her own heated response. She couldn't believe what was happening to her.

'Jen, I've got to get away,' she announced huskily. 'I need time to ... to think. I've told my agent to tell them I'm not interested in the Rio contract.' She saw Jennifer's expression and smiled. 'Yes I know, I've left it a bit late in the day, but I thought I'd try to get away somewhere, concentrate on my writing. . . .'

'You mean run away from Race,' Jennifer said acidly, 'where will you go?'

'I've no idea. Somewhere remote and quiet. Let me know if you get any ideas.'

'You know you were saying about going away, Heather?'

Heather raised her head from her newspaper to glance at her cousin. Three days had passed since she had seen Race; three days during which her stomach had clenched each time the telephone rang or someone knocked on the door, but he had made no attempt to get in touch with her. That didn't mean that he never would; she was sure he was just biding his time, waiting. . . . He had known she had responded to him. She couldn't disguise that and like any hunter smelling blood he would track her down, pursuing his kill.

'Do you still want to? Get away, I mean?'

Surprised Heather nodded her head. Jennifer had been totally against her going away when she first mentioned it. 'Why?' she asked. 'I thought you disapproved.'

'Mm. . . . Well perhaps you ought to if it's what you really want. It's just that Terry has this cottage in the Highlands of Scotland. He uses it during the summer for fishing, and I'm sure he'd lend it to you if you wanted him to. He was talking about it yesterday, that's what gave me the idea.' She flushed as Heather looked at her. 'I'm only trying to help,' she assured her, 'but if you don't like the idea. . . . '

The Scottish Highlands, all grim grandeur and sullen skies; the scenery suited her mood. 'Have you discussed it with Terry?' she asked.

Jennifer shook her head. 'Not yet, but I'm sure he won't mind. I'll ask him tomorrow if you like.' She seemed unnaturally tense, and Heather wondered if Race Williams had been questioning her again. Jennifer hadn't mentioned him and Heather hadn't asked.

'It sounds tempting,' she admitted.

'Oh, Heather,' Jennifer's eyes were shadowed, 'are you sure you're doing the right thing? Why don't you stay here, talk to Race. . . .'

Stay and let him overwhelm her defences again? Never! She had to get away, she wasn't strong enough to stay and fight. There was something about him that robbed her of her invincibility; she feared him and she feared the way he made her feel.

'I can't,' she told Jennifer huskily, 'I must get away. Ask Terry if I can use his cottage. Tell him I want peace and quiet to work on my book. After all, it isn't a lie. . . .'

'Well, if you're sure. . .?'

Heather frowned. Why was Jennifer hesitating. She had been the one to bring up the subject, and now that she was agreeing she seemed to be hanging back, trying to get her to change her mind. Probably because she was romantic enough to believe her own P.R. work on Race's behalf. She wouldn't put it past Jennifer to actually convince herself that he did feel something more than lust for her, but she knew that wasn't true. No man with any real feelings could have behaved the way he had.

CHAPTER THREE

'FOR heaven's sake stop worrying! Of course it's all right, but Terry said to warn you that you could find yourself snowed in, so take plenty of provisions. Fortunately the cottage has its own generator and all mod cons, so you needn't worry about that aspect too much.'

'And it's perfectly all right for me to use the cottage? He doesn't mind?'

'Look, I've already told you a dozen times that he doesn't,' Jennifer said in exasperation. 'Here's the key, and I've rung Mum and she says you can borrow her Mini. She's going to drive it up to Town on Sunday and stay over to do some shopping; check up on us both, so on Saturday we'll go shopping.'

Her cousin was displaying a remarkable aptitude for organisation all of a sudden, Heather reflected wryly, listening to Jennifer. The more she thought about Terry's cottage, the more it appealed. She had never been to Scotland; she could even perhaps set some of her novel there. She was planning a factional work, a blend of fact and fiction, using as her base the de Travers family who for centuries had been the local squires of the village where Heather's aunt and uncle lived. The family had died out during the first world war, but the Hall was still there and the local library abounded with information about the family. Heather had been fascinated by their history for as long as she could remember and knew it off by heart. They had come over to England with Henry II, and their history was closely entwined with that of England, but the information she had about them was not so detailed that she couldn't embroider relationships where she wanted to.

The week passed without her hearing from Race, but that didn't lessen her acute state of anxiety. She had lost weight and her nerves were so on edge that even Jennifer had noticed. She could hardly sit still and felt as though she were living on top of a live bomb, just waiting for it to go off. She felt vulnerable, afraid, tense to the point of hysteria. Remembering how she had felt in his arms kept her awake at night.

Jennifer didn't help either. On several occasions she had pleaded with Heather to change her mind about her trip to Scotland, veering from seeming pleased that she was going to almost begging her not to do so. Heather half suspected her cousin of playing the devil's advocate, or being primed by Race, but once she got to Scotland she would be safe. It was too far for him to follow her; he couldn't leave his new position as head of the Documentary Department on Southern Television, not so soon after taking it up, and she began to long for the sanctuary the cottage had come to represent.

She was planning to leave that weekend, and was just deciding what to take with her when she heard Jennifer's key in the lock.

'You're home early.'

'Um, my boss gave me time off. He's taking me out to dinner tonight. Well, actually he wants to take us both out. Don't look like that,' she told Heather, 'it isn't a trick to get you to meet Race. Terry wants to talk, about the cottage, either that or he thinks he needs a chaperon to protect him from me,' she joked, giggling as she added provocatively, 'and he'd be right. I love him, Heather,' she went on more quietly, 'and I think he suspects it—damn him. No, he wants to see you tonight to make sure you know the way to the cottage, and, I suspect, to check that I wasn't lying when I told him you weren't a featherbrain like me.'

Terry picked them up at eight and drove them to a new Italian restaurant run by some friends of his. The atmosphere was friendly and relaxing, and Heather found herself responding quite naturally to his questions. She had always liked him, and suspected he was by no means as indifferent to her cousin as he pretended.

'I've already mapped out a route,' Heather told him when they reached the sweet course, showing it to him. 'Jen's warned me about stocking up with food etc. My aunt is lending me her Mini for the journey.'

'A Mini? Umm. . . . The weather can be pretty devastating up there, you could quite easily find yourself snowed in, but Jen tells me you aren't frightened of your own company.'

'Not in the least,' Heather assured him, asking quickly, 'Have you owned the cottage long?'

He shook his head. 'Not very, a couple of years, that's all. I only have a half share in it, I bought it with a friend and we both tend to use it as a retreat. There's only one bedroom, so we've come to a satisfactory agreement about timing our visits and it works quite well.'

'Pity it's only got one bedroom,' Jennifer broke in roguishly. 'I was going to suggest you took me up with you next time you go.'

'Perhaps I will,' Terry agreed, his eyes teasing as he added, 'You could always sleep downstairs on the settee.'

Mmm, not indifferent to her cousin at all, Heather thought in amusement, but wise enough not to make the chase too easy for her. Jen could well find out that she'd taken on more than she'd bargained for. 'Come on, girls, I'd better take you home,' he added. 'I've got to be at the studio at six tomorrow morning. Think yourself lucky you don't work Saturdays,' he told Jennifer, adding to Heather. 'By the way, there's no phone at the cottage, although there is a farm with one about four or five miles away.'

Saturday was busy. They shopped in the morning, the mound of tinned and dried food stacked in the kitchen after their forays, making Heather wonder how she would get it all in the Mini.

'Dried milk, flour, coffee, tea, butter, eggs—that's the essentials at least,' Jennifer commented ticking them off on their list, 'and then you've all these tins.'

'Mmm, they'll do for the days when I'm too busy writing to stop to prepare a proper meal. Terry did say there was an emergency Calor gas stove in case the generator failed, didn't he?'

'Yes, and plenty of logs. Sounds rather primitive to me. Are you sure you want to go?'

'Positive,' Heather told her firmly. 'In fact I'm looking forward to it. Now, what else? Oh, I mustn't forget all my research books and my papers.'

'Keep on going at this rate and you won't have any room for your clothes,' Jennifer told her sarcastically. 'Let's get some lunch and then we'll go out again. What else do you need?' She glanced at her list.

'Some thermal underwear might be a good idea,' Heather joked, 'especially if I do get snowed in.'

'You need new jeans,' Jennifer told her, 'and new sweaters. You can't go on wearing the twins' cast-offs for ever. I know a shop that stocks the most adorable hand-knits with the cutest designs on them.'

'No doubt at the most adorable prices,' Heather agreed, suppressing a sigh. She had been thinking more along the lines of chain-store clothes.

By the end of the afternoon her feet and legs were exhausted. Jennifer must have dragged her through every shop in London. She had spent far too much money—nearly all her Christmas cheque from her aunt and uncle, and all she had to show for it was half a dozen jumpers, two new pairs of cords, and some sensible fleecy-lined wellington boots, plus a thick padded jacket with a hood. She turned round, looking for Jennifer, grimacing faintly as she realised her cousin had disappeared yet again.

'Here I am,' Jennifer announced, touching her arm. 'Just buying you a little goodbye prezzy.' She was grinning, and Heather wondered uneasily what she had bought. They were back in the flat before she found out, gasping as she saw the delicate satin and lace underwear Jennifer spread out for her inspection. 'Oh Jen, they must have cost the earth,' she protested. 'And there's no use saying you don't want them. The shop won't take them back, and they won't fit me. Look,' Jennifer coaxed, 'you'll be wearing jeans and jumpers all the time you're up there. Indulge yourself a little. There's nothing for making you feel all woman like wearing sexy undies.'

'Perhaps I don't want to feel "all woman",' Heather told her tartly. She'd experienced enough of that particular feeling to last a lifetime in Race Williams' arms, but Jen had only meant to be kind and it seemed churlish to refuse her gift, even though the delicate fabric and brevity of the garments she had bought would be completely out of place in the cottage environment, and totally impractical.

'Mum should be here soon,' Jennifer told her as they prepared the evening meal. 'We'll load the Mini tonight, so you can get an early start.'

True to Jennifer's prediction, her mother arrived just as she was putting the finishing touches to the

table. She kissed both girls warmly, stretching up to
hug Heather, both of them laughing. Like Jennifer,
her mother was small and dainty, and when the two of
them were together Heather felt like a giantess. 'It's
freezing out there,' Lydia Murray announced as
Heather served the soup. 'Are you sure you're doing
the right thing, Heather? I'll worry about you, driving
all that way.' That was one of the nice things about her
aunt, Heather thought warmly. She never differ-
entiated between her own children and Heather, her
love for all of them was unbounding. 'I can't
understand why you want to go to Scotland,' she
fretted.

'She's running away,' Jennifer said mischievously,
adding with a sly grin at her cousin, 'from a man.'

Her mother looked startled. 'Jennifer!' she expostulated as though unable to believe what Jennifer was
telling her.

'I said a man, Mother, that's a . . . M-A-N.' She
rolled her eyes and laughed. 'You know, the sort that
makes you weak at the knees, a bit like Clark Gable,'
she teased her flustered parent, 'and he's finally made
Heather realise that she's human. Heather,' she
announced, disregarding the bleak look Heather was
giving her, 'has finally woken up and discovered sex
appeal—with a vengeance—and now she's running
away.'

'Jen, you mustn't tease Heather like that,' her
mother protested, 'and I'm sure she's doing no such
thing. She's far too sensible.'

Sensible! A wry smile twisted Heather's mouth. If
only her aunt knew! All her life, because of her height
and more serious nature, she had been dubbed
'sensible' and 'practical', but since her meeting with
Race Williams she had been feeling neither of those
things—far from it. And Jennifer was far too acute.

She was glad she was getting away from London, she wouldn't put it past her to try and engineer another meeting between them if she stayed. Of course she wouldn't do it from malice, Jen wasn't like that, but to her there could be nothing more logical than for Heather to want to pursue her acquaintanship with Race. Jennifer thought her reluctance to see him again sprang from embarrassment and the discovery that she wasn't immune to him. Her cousin had no conception of the fear and anguish rioting inside her; the sheer terror she experienced each time she remembered how he had made her feel. As long ago as adolescence she had told herself that no man was ever going to have the power to hurt her ever again, and that was the way it had been until . . . until Race Williams touched her and sent her up in flames, all her carefully constructed barriers turned to ashes at her feet.

She went to bed early, knowing she was going to have a long drive ahead of her, and was touched when both her aunt and Jennifer got up to have breakfast with her, coming to wave her off as she headed north.

Once on the motorway some of the tension that had been with her since she woke up disappeared. There had been a sharp drop in temperature overnight and she drove carefully, taking her time, stopping for lunch just before she reached the Lake District, the quiet village pub she found almost deserted.

The food and rest replenished her energy, but she hadn't realised just how far she was going to have to drive, she reflected ruefully as she glanced at the snow-covered peaks of the Cumbrian mountains, brief flurries of snow dancing against the windscreen. The further north she got, the worse the weather, and when she eventually pulled off the motorway she felt concerned enough to check at the motel she came to, on the state of the roads and the weather forecast.

'We've had it bad,' the pump attendant told her. 'Heavy snowfalls twice this last week, and they say there's been more up past Fort William, but the roads are still open. Where are you going?' Heather gave him the name of the village closest to the cottage. 'Mmm—it's pretty remote up there, hang on a sec, I'll check with the weather centre. Why don't you go and get yourself a cup of coffee, it won't take long.' When Heather thanked him he shrugged. 'Better to be safe than sorry. We get too many inexperienced motorists coming up here, not realising how severe the weather can be. That last bad winter several lives were lost, partially through carelessness. Come back in about a quarter of an hour and I should have found out something for you.'

The coffee she ordered came quickly and was hot and reviving. After fifteen minutes had passed Heather returned apprehensively to the forecourt. Having come all this way she didn't fancy having to turn back.

'You're in luck,' the attendant told her. 'But I hope you're planning more than a weekend stay? There's a blizzard on the way. Should hit tomorrow, so you've got plenty of time to get there.'

Thanking him for his kindness, Heather paused to check her tyres. She wasn't going to take any chances. He smiled approvingly at her as she drove off, giving her the confidence to hold the small car steady on the thin black ribbon of road, alarmingly bordered by unending vistas of white.

It was dark before she reached Fort William, barely pausing there in her anxiety to reach her destination. She thought about staying overnight and then remembered what the garage attendant had said about the blizzard. It would be better to finish her journey tonight, tired though she was than risk having to turn back in the morning. And besides, it was only another twenty miles or so.

They must be the twenty longest miles in existence, Heather thought tiredly after what seemed like hours of driving through the darkness; the road almost deserted, the white silence of the countryside around her; the starkness of the scenery all combining to make her unusually edgy and nervous, Ben Nevis and the surrounding mountains towering above her, the pass along which her small car crawled unnervingly deserted. At last she found the signpost for the village, disturbed to find the road climbing steeply, but fortunately free from the snow which was banked high either side of her. The village, when she eventually came to it, was no more than a small cluster of houses, and a small shop, and garage, the latter illuminated. Thankfully Heather pulled into the forecourt. She wasn't going any further until she had made absolutely sure of her directions. Even as she opened the door snow started to whirl down around her, and the man who emerged from the small office was quickly covered in the thick flakes as he strode towards her.

'So it's the MacDonald cottage you'll be wanting?' he asked in the soft sing-song of the Highlands. 'I doubt you'll get there in your Mini, lassie. The road's been closed these two days past.' Something of her disappointment must have shown on her face, because he said, 'I'm not promising, mind, but it may be that the Land Rover will make it. Staying long?'

'Two months,' Heather told him. 'It belongs to a friend of my cousin's. I'm—I'm a writer. . . .' she added, feeling that some explanation for her sudden appearance was necessary. She knew all about village life and village curiosity from the Cotswolds where her aunt and uncle lived.

'If you'll just bide a while I'll close up here and

we'll load your stuff into the Land Rover. Come well prepared have you?' He peered into the Mini and grunted approval as he opened the boot. 'Aye, it's a good seven mile on foot down here to Mrs Mac's shop, but I see you'll not starve. A writer, you say . . . now there's a coincidence.' He didn't say what the coincidence was, as he lifted one of the large cardboard boxes from the back seat of the Mini and deposited it in the battered Land Rover. 'I'll garage the Mini down here for you,' he offered, 'get someone to bring it up when the weather lifts. Who did you say your friend was?' he added gently, but Heather wasn't deceived and hid a small smile, knowing he was checking up on her, and why not? It was all part of the obvious neighbourliness of the villagers.

'My cousin works with Terry Brady,' Heather explained. 'He and a friend own the cottage.'

'Aye, that's right. Comes up for fishing, does Terry. Nice laddie. Come on up with you,' he added, hoisting Heather into the Land Rover and then slamming the door.

The battered vehicle was cold, and Heather shivered as he got in beside her, wishing she was wearing the thick padded jacket packed away in her case. 'I had no idea the weather was going to be as bad as this,' she told him. 'I stopped in Cumbria and they told me a blizzard was forecast—for tomorrow.'

'Aye, like as not,' her companion agreed laconically, engaging four-wheel-drive as they chugged out of the forecourt.

The road to the cottage was steep and ankle deep in snow, deeper in parts, but the Land Rover, although sliding occasionally, causing her stomach muscles to tense made light of the hill in a way that was far beyond the capabilities of her poor aunt's Mini. As they drove the snow started to come down more heavily, thickly covering the windscreen blotting out the landscape. The road dipped and then rose again and as the wipers cleared the window she had a glimpse of a sheet of water glittering under the stars. 'Yon's the loch,' she was told impassively. 'The cottage is only a step away now.'

The step was about a mile, and Heather gritted her teeth as they bumped down what could only have been a farm track and which Terry had failed to mention. In the headlights of the Land Rover the cottage huddled against the hillside, dark and unwelcoming. She opened her bag looking for her key as they came to a stop. Her companion, who had introduced himself as Fergus, was already lifting the boxes from the back of the Land Rover, shaking his head when she offered to help him, indicating that she go ahead and unlock the door.

Surprisingly the house felt quite warm, the door opening straight on to an old-fashioned kitchen, complete with a stone floor and large scrubbed table. 'Oh, aye, that will be Mrs MacNeil from the farm,' Fergus told her when she expressed surprise. 'She'll have sent someone down to switch on the heating, keep the place from freezing.' He also told her that the cottage had once belonged to the MacNeils but that they had sold it. As soon as the weather clears I'll tell them you're here,' he offered, adding doubtfully, 'Are you sure you want to stay?'

Did she? For a moment Heather felt doubtful, and then she reminded herself that it was pointless coming all this way to back out at the last minute. The generator was obviously working. Fergus had switched on the lights. The house was warm and would undoubtedly get warmer if she turned up the thermostat. She had nothing to fear, unless it was her own company, whereas if she returned to London. . . .

'I'll be fine,' she assured him. 'I'd offer you a cup of tea, but I don't know where everything is yet. You must let me pay you for your petrol, though.'

Firmly refusing both offers, he brought in the rest of her belongings, and when the tail lights of the Land Rover finally disappeared into the swirling snow, Heather felt an acute sense of loneliness.

An hour later she had unpacked and explored. The cupboards were surprisingly well stocked; even down to half open packets of cereal and fresh food in the fridge. Perhaps the farmer's wife kept it stocked for Terry and his co-owner, or perhaps Terry had telephoned and asked her to stock it for her. The living room was surprisingly large, furnished attractively in natural fabrics and furniture in soft greens and browns. An open staircase led up to the second floor; the bathroom, and the single bedroom Terry had described. Curiously for such an isolated and seldom used cottage, the rooms had a lived in air which was vaguely comforting.

Downstairs again, Heather made herself a drink and surveyed her cases. She would unpack those tomorrow. She was feeling acutely tired and suddenly longed to go to bed. Back in the living room she studied the table, wondering whether it would be best to work from here or from the kitchen. Her typewriter lay on the floor in its case, and she noticed an empty space on the bookshelves running along from the fire and decided she might as well store it there until the morning. A cupboard beneath the shelves was locked, and she wondered why as she placed her typewriter on the shelf. The shelves also housed an expensive hi-fi system; far too expensive to only be used on the odd weeks in the year when the cottage was lived in.

Heather went to the window and peered out. The snow was coming down very heavily, the wind picking up. Shivering, she checked that everything was put away and then picked up her cases, wondering if the heating also produced hot water. Right at this moment she could think of nothing more attractive than a hot bath, followed by a very long sleep.

Some time during the night she woke up, wondering what had disturbed her, and if she had really imagined the sound of a Land Rover engine. She must have done, she decided several minutes later, when the only sound to break the silence was her own heartbeat. She must have been dreaming about the drive up here.

Well, she had done it. She had escaped. Now she could put Race Williams well and truly behind her and concentrate on the job in hand. Her book.

CHAPTER FOUR

IT was the unusual clarity of the light that woke her, piercing her closed eyes, making her blink dopily as she stared towards the window. Last night she had forgotten to close the curtains. Pushing aside the comforting warmth of the duvet cover, she noticed that the pillow next to her own was also dented as though she had slept restlessly; as indeed she had done ever since she met Race Williams, but last night she thought she had slept unusually well; she even had a vague memory of feeling extraordinarily warm and safe. Leaving the bed, she padded to the window, lost in delight at the scene below. Everything was white; a deep dense white, not a thing moved. At first she was too entranced by the view to notice the menace of the snow clouds piled up on the horizon, shivering suddenly as she became aware of the biting cold outside the bed. Of the road she had travelled along last night there was no sign, and she caught her breath in the realisation that it was completely blocked, invisible under the deep cover of snow which had piled up round the house in huge drifts. Even as she watched fresh flakes started to fall from the sky, gathering in momentum, whirling and tumbling earthwards, tossed and tormented by the wind she could hear keening across the landscape.

A faint click behind her made her turn, her face as white as the scenery outside as she saw the man standing with his back to the door, bare, hair-darkened legs visible beneath the hem of a navy towelling robe, his hair damp as though he had recently showered, a tray with two mugs of coffee on it balanced on one hand.

'So you're awake, then. I thought you were going to sleep for ever.'

Against her will Heather's eyes were drawn back to the bed; the intimacy of the thick duvet, the two pillows both dented; the discarded clothes on the chair she hadn't noticed before. She took a deep breath, trying to force down the panic she could feel welling up inside her. For a moment she thought she must have been hallucinating, but no, he was here all right—very much in the flesh—watching her with those cool grey eyes that saw far too much.

'Don't I even get a "good morning"?'

Heather shivered, knowing he was mocking her, a thousand bitter questions clamouring for utterance, but the only words she found her tongue could form, a whispered, 'You tricked me!'

He was actually here in this room with her, the man she had run so far away from. His robe fell open as he leaned down to put the tray on a small table and she was burningly aware that beneath the terrycloth he was naked, and she knew he had intended her to be aware of it. The thought ran through her mind that Jennifer must have known about this, and not just known but actually abetted. Silly, romantic Jen, who probably thought she was doing her some sort of favour.

'Your cousin seems to think we're sort of star-crossed lovers,' he mocked, shocking her with the clarity with which he read her mind.

'Because you encouraged her to believe it,' Heather said huskily. Her throat was dry with angry tension. How could she have been so stupid? There had been several signs that everything was not as it should be. Jen had asked her several times if she really wanted to come up here, suffering from the pangs of guilty conscience, no doubt, and giving her the opportunity to back out; and Terry, too, had been nervous, over-cheerful when he took them out to dinner.

'Why?' she demanded angrily at last. 'Why go to all this trouble? There must be dozens of women who. . . .'

'I could take to bed?' he supplied for her, patently completely unaffected by her rage. 'Of course, but you see, I wanted you. From the first moment I saw you when your agent submitted your portfolio for the Rio contract. Terry and I have been friends for years, and when I found out about you and Jennifer I decided it would be better to organise an introduction through her rather than use my position with Rio. Why did you back out of the contract, by the way?' he asked softly, watching her.

Dear God, he was always watching her following every movement of her body with those steel-grey eyes, making her acutely conscious of the thin fabric of her nightdress, and the vulnerability of her body beneath it.

'Did you think I wouldn't after you'd tried to bribe me?' Heather demanded fiercely. 'Do you honestly think I would want the contract on those terms? I've never used my body in that way, never . . . and I never will.'

'But you've used it to drive men mad, haven't you, Heather?' he demanded softly. 'You've used it to blind and bind them before you finally destroy their egos. It's time someone taught you a lesson, showed you that there are times when you just can't win; you just can't give men the sort of come-on you deal in and then kick them in the face. It isn't going to be like that with me. I've got you running scared, haven't I? When Jennifer told me what you were going to do, that you wanted to leave London, to get away to "write", I knew immediately what I was going to do.'

He was gloating over her, revelling in his underhand manoeuvring of her, and Heather felt anger pulse through her. 'Is that the kind of man you are, a man who can only get what he wants by deceit and cheating? Terry lied to me—he told me he owned this cottage with a friend.'

'Which he does,' Race told her, 'me, and if it makes you feel any better I had to work hard to persuade him to help me. He thinks I'm a fellow victim of cupid's dart,' he told her, smiling ferally, 'and so, reluctantly, he gave in.'

'And now you've got me here what do you plan to do with me?' Heather asked, forcing down her hysteria. 'Rape me?'

'That's what you'd like me to do, isn't it?' Race answered sardonically. 'That way you get to reinforce your hatred of my sex; because you do hate us, don't you, Heather? And you use your looks and your body to exact your own subtle revenge upon us. Why, I wonder?'

He was too astute; too able to see into her mind. She looked out of the window, her heart sinking when she saw the falling snow. She couldn't stay here, not with this man; he would destroy her, she knew it, and it wasn't merely physical capitulation that she feared, but something far, far more dangerous.

And he meant to break her, Heather knew that. Why else would he go to such lengths, even to the extent of making sure he wasn't there last night when she arrived, so that she couldn't leave? But she would leave. It was only a few miles to the village, she would do anything to get away from this man—anything.

'I'm leaving,' she told him huskily. 'The moment I'm dressed I'm going.'

'You can't. The drifts are over twenty feet deep on the way down to the village, and there's a blizzard forecast. You'd freeze before you got more than a mile. Try it if you like, but I'll come after you, and of the two of us I have the greater stamina. At heart you're just a coward, aren't you?' he taunted. 'Why are you so frightened of me? I'm just another man, right? Just another victim to be tortured and tormented. Oh yes, I've heard all about it, about how you just love to emasculate your victims. What's so different about me? Or are you scared I might break through to the real woman—that's what you're frightened of, isn't it, Heather. Not me, but yourself. All those other men, none of them really touched you, not the real you. Oh, they might have possessed your body, but that was all, and you used it to lure them on to their own destruction, didn't you?'

He was too astute, too frighteningly able to grasp all that she would rather keep hidden from him.

'Yes,' she admitted on a tortured breath. 'Yes, yes, yes . . . but it won't be any different with you, Race, no matter what you think. I didn't run away from you,' she lied. 'I came up here because I wanted to work, because I was sick and tired of men who thought they could buy me—men like you,' she told him dangerously. 'You can keep me here by force, you can take my body by force, but I don't want you and I'll never want you.'

'Then I'll have to make you, won't I?' he said softly. His eyes dropped to her breasts and Heather had a momentary and completely unnerving recollection of how she had felt when he had touched them. Something seemed to melt and dissolve inside her and she knew she was trembling.

'You're going to come to me willingly, I promise you that now,' she heard Race saying to her above the thunder of her heartbeat. He was breathing heavily, his features taut, the grey eyes burning feverishly as they moved across her body, and then, so suddenly that the release of pressure was almost tangible, he added, 'Drink your coffee while it's still hot, and I shouldn't linger up here too long if I were you, this room isn't centrally heated. In fact if the blizzard persists, I'm not too sure how long the generator will last out. We won't freeze, though,' he told her, 'there's a fire downstairs and we've got plenty of logs, and we can always keep one another warm in bed at night.'

Heather stared at the double bed, as she knew he had intended her to do. 'I'm not sharing that bed with you!'

'Perhaps not tonight,' he agreed, 'but I'm no gentleman, Heather, and I'm not giving it up for you. You'll soon find out that when it's a choice between freezing or being warm, you'll opt for the latter, and that will be your choice.'

He left before she could say anything, and Heather heard the sound of water running in the bathroom. How could she have got herself in this situation? How could Jen have helped him? She sighed, already knowing the answer to that question. Poor, romantic, deluded Jennifer, she had no conception of what Race really wanted.

But did she? Heather frowned, absently picking up the mug of coffee and curling her fingers round it. It was almost diabolical how he had manoeuvred her into this situation, even the weather had worked against her. She glanced out into the snow. Twenty-foot drifts, he had said, and she suspected he hadn't been lying. She couldn't see the ground now for the dense snowflakes, and the thought of walking the seven miles to the village was, she knew, in her heart of hearts, suicide, but if she stayed. . . .

It came to her that all she had to do was to tell him the truth, to admit that she wasn't the woman of experience he thought and that she was, in fact, still a virgin. She was pretty sure if she did she would be safe, but her pride wouldn't let her admit it to him; if she did he would know why she had run, he would know exactly why she feared him and the intensely sexual response of her senses to him.

Her body wanted him as its lover. There! She had admitted it to herself at last, she had known it the first moment she saw him. Even while she loathed him mentally her body had responded to the lure of his, and he, damn him, had sensed it, and that was why he was so determined to pursue her, she was sure of it. That plus the challenge of making her give to him what he sensed she had not given to anyone else, a physical response. Race had said he wouldn't force her, and Heather felt he had probably spoken the truth. He wanted her to go to him and was sure enough of his sexual power to believe she would do so. After all, as far as he knew she was a woman with considerable sexual experience, a woman who probably, to his male mind, would not miss the challenge of taking a new lover. And that being the case he would probably look to her to make the first overtures. Provided the snow went quickly she was probably perfectly safe. Provided the snow went and she could withstand the assault of his masculinity on her senses. She mustn't delude herself. She was dangerously at risk where he was concerned, why else had she left London in the first place?

Heather heard the bathroom door open and tensed as Race walked into the bedroom.

'I'd advise you to wear something warm,' he warned her, walking over to a set of drawers and removing socks and underpants. 'The heating is working, but not at full efficiency.'

Even when he was talking normally without the relentless sexual pressure she had grown used to, there was still a maleness about him that tormented her senses, and she was glad of the old camel dressing-gown which she had put on in his absence, glad that those too-knowing grey eyes couldn't linger on her body. The dressing gown had once belonged to Rick, one of the twins, and she had brought it with her on impulse. Now she was glad she had done so, and trying to match his casual air she extracted clean clothes from her case and hurried into the bathroom, relieved to notice that it possessed a bolt.

She was too tense to linger under the shower, disturbed by the way her hands trembled as she pulled on her new cords and a toning fleecy jumper. As was her habit when she wasn't working, she didn't bother with any make-up, simply brushing her hair and securing it at her nape before returning to the bedroom, glad to find that it was empty. Neat and tidy by nature, she found herself smoothing the sheets and plumping up the pillows almost by habit, shaking the duvet before she returned it to the bed, some sixth sense warning her that Race had returned, even before she straightened and saw him.

'Very domesticated,' he mocked, watching the colour film her face with almost detached interest. 'It won't work, Heather,' he told her slowly when he had finished studying her body. 'Oh, I appreciate that you might think tying back your hair and going without make-up is a turn-off, but believe me, *I* don't think so—far from it. In your make-up you're an exceptionally beautiful and sexy woman. Without it, though, there's an earthy sensuality about you far more potent than any amount of cosmetics.'

The gall of him! Did he actually think she hadn't worn make-up because of him? Grinding her teeth,

Heather walked past him and picked up her mug and the tray.

'In case you've forgotten,' she said pointedly from the door, 'I came here to work, and that's exactly what I intend to do.'

'Your book,' he agreed, nodding his head. 'That's fine by me, I'm working on one myself at the moment.' He saw her expression and smiled. 'Oh, I'm not lying. My business interests are fairly diverse now, but I do still write. That's one of the reasons I bought this place. I'd intended coming up here anyway, and when I learned you were looking for a bolt-hole. . . .'

'I'm surprised you bothered,' Heather said with heavy irony. 'I shouldn't have thought you would want the distraction.'

He laughed at that. 'Poor Heather, you're in for a slight disappointment if you expect me to spend all day trying to coax you into my bed. When I'm working nothing distracts me, but you're perfectly welcome to try.'

Still grinding her teeth, Heather went downstairs. In the daylight the living room still looked as attractive as it had done the previous night, and was pleasantly warm. Some papers and a typewriter lay on the large table, as though to confirm that Race hadn't been joking when he said he intended to work. Well, that suited her fine. Anger bubbled inside her, but behind the anger lay fear, and it took all her strength of will to force herself to walk calmly across to where she had put her own typewriter and reference books and carry them through into the kitchen.

'I've had my breakfast, but you'd better have something to eat before you start work.'

Race moved exceptionally silently for so large a man. She hadn't heard him coming downstairs, and she jumped nervously, the books she had piled into her arms falling on to the floor.

'My, my, you are jumpy aren't you?' He bent and picked them up for her, the dark hair ruffled at the back of his head, his neck brown against the checked shirt he was wearing. A curious melting sensation spread through her body, and she had to force herself not to react as he stood up, piling the books back into her arms, his fingers brushing the tips of her breasts—deliberately, she was quite sure, although he gave no indication of having touched her. It would have been quite easy for him to carry the books he had picked up through into the kitchen for her, but no, he had to give them back to her, to touch her, her body registering the contact with every nerve ending.

How on earth had she ever thought of herself as cold? She was burning up inside with the need to reach out and touch him, to slide her palms against the taut warmth of his chest, to taste the tanned male flesh.

'What's your book about?' He stepped casually away from her, releasing her from the spell of his proximity, allowing her mind to function without being clouded by the responses of her body. This can't be happening to me, she thought feverishly. No man makes me feel like this. No man. But Race was, and she was sure he knew it.

She shuddered deeply, no longer sure of her ability to keep him at bay. But she must. She had to.

'A family saga,' she told him huskily. 'I haven't started it properly yet.'

'But you've obviously done a considerable amount of research. It's historical, I take it?' He sounded so genuinely interested, so calm and friendly that she couldn't equate him with the man who had stood watching her earlier, telling her that she would go to him—willingly. She couldn't take this constant seesawing on her emotions, Heather thought tiredly; Race changed too rapidly for her, making her mind ache with the effort of keeping pace with him.

She wasn't hungry, but she forced herself to eat some of the cereal she had brought with her, all the time conscious of him moving about in the other room, jumping when she heard the staccato sound of his typewriter. God, her nerves were in a dreadful state if something like that made her jump! She was tense, too tense, her mind wound up to breaking point. She washed up her bowl and cutlery, trying to force herself to think about her book, willing herself backwards in time, trying to imagine what it must have been like to live then, trying to feel the emotions of her characters.

'I'm just going outside to check the generator.'

Once again Race had caught her off guard, her eyes following him as he walked to the door and paused to pull on wellingtons and a thick hooded jacket. When he opened the door she gasped at the inrush of cold air and thick flakes of snow. The snow had drifted against the door, and he reached for a spade that was leaning up where his coat had been. 'The MacNeils warned me about this last night when I was up there,' he told her casually, as he bent to shovel away the snow. 'Luckily he managed to get all his sheep in first. . . .'

The MacNeils. That was where he had been when she arrived, waiting . . . knowing. . . . Heather shivered, and it wasn't purely because of the cold air filling the kitchen. Her eyes were drawn to the breadth of his back, the effortless way in which he removed the snow, almost hypnotised by the rhythmic movements of his body. The snow was deeper than she had expected, and it was plain that he would have to clear a path to get to the shed which housed the generator. Perhaps she ought to offer to help?

She did, hesitatingly, and was surprised by the look of amusement in his eyes. 'What's the matter?' he mocked. 'Are you afraid I'll get lost out there and you'll be left all alone?'

Muttering under her breath that she wished he would, Heather picked one of her books and started studying it, ignoring the sounds from outside, trying to blot out her awareness of him. He had closed the door and she could see nothing. How long would it take him to dig through to the hut? She glanced at her watch, trying to fight down her growing sense of anxiety as twenty minutes and then half an hour went by. It was silly really, all she had to do was to go and open the door to see where he was, but pride wouldn't let her, her imagination tormenting her with pictures of him instead. Could he have hurt himself?

Panic flared and she clamped down on it. The light she had switched on to work flickered suddenly and she glanced apprehensively towards the door, mentally cursing herself when it opened and Race walked in, stamping the snow off his boots, shaking his head and dislodging flakes of snow and moisture, the sound and sight of him filling the kitchen, the air crisp with the scent of outdoors, mingling with the healthy male smell of his body.

'I don't think the generator can last out much longer,' he told her, removing his jacket. 'I'll go out later and bring in the logs. Luckily they're dry and there are plenty of them, but the fire will only heat the living room.'

When he had finished removing his boots and jacket he came over to her, standing behind her chair, leaning forward until she could feel his cold breath against the back of her neck as he bent to read the title of her book, hands resting either side of her on the desk, enclosing her, making her vulnerably aware of everything about him. She froze instinctively, knowing that he was doing it deliberately, playing on her emotions.

'We ought to organise some sort of rota,' he surprised her by saying, 'for the chores. How about me doing lunch today and you doing dinner, and then tomorrow we'll get something sorted out?'

Heather hid her surprise, nodding her head. She wasn't used to men who talked casually about 'doing the chores'. Neither her uncle nor the twins ever lifted a finger at home, and she wasn't on intimate terms with the other men she knew enough to know how domesticated or otherwise they were. Race had a strength about him that refused to be quelled, an implacability she could not fight. It was like a solid iron wall. That was why he kept on insisting that she wanted him. He couldn't possibly know how she felt, and she wasn't going to let him find out. Dear God, to think she had come all this way, running away from him! She glanced out at the snow-covered landscape which had afforded her so much pleasure when she first woke up. Now she would give anything for the snow to disappear and for her to be able to walk out of the door. However, far from disappearing, if anything it was snowing even harder, she noticed as she walked into the kitchen, and the wind had picked up too, the fierce keening sound making her shiver, despite the warmth of her clothes and the cottage.

She filled the kettle, switching it on and glancing into the other room where she could see Race's dark head bent over some papers on the table. Should she offer to make him a cup? Wasn't it more sensible to try and build up some sort of working relationship rather than endure open warfare? She found one of the jars of coffee she had brought with her and tried to open it, but the top resisted all her efforts, her wrist aching as she refused to give in. The kettle was boiling and she glanced wrathfully at the recalcitrant jar, placing it on the table with a thump while she went to switch off the kettle.

'Having problems?' She hadn't heard Race come into the kitchen. He picked up the jar, releasing the lid with an effortless ease that made Heather shiver, thinking of the power and strength in those lean fingers. He smiled mirthlessly at her, as though he had read her mind and offered tauntingly, 'Some things call for subtlety—not brute strength. How tall are you, by the way?' he added, bringing a rich tide of colour to her face as he surveyed her. 'Six foot?'

Heather's mouth compressed. 'Five ten, actually,' she told him, picking up the jar and removing a mug from the cupboard.

He didn't say anything else, but Heather was left with the impression that he knew how acutely conscious she was about her height. Strangely enough, instead of making her hunch into herself, the gibe had the effect of making her consciously stretch her body proudly, her eyes brilliantly emerald against the paleness of her face as she spooned coffee into her mug.

'Would you like a cup?'

Race nodded and she went to get another mug, wondering why every time he stepped into a room it suddenly seemed to shrink. He took his coffee back to the table and soon became engrossed in what he was doing. Heather went back to her own typewriter and books, settling herself in the kitchen, and then checking the fridge to see what she could make for their evening meal. In the end she decided on a casserole. Her aunt was an excellent cook and had passed her skill on to both her daughter and her niece, and as she sliced vegetables for the casserole, her movements economically deft, Heather found her tensed muscles gradually starting to relax. She didn't think she would ever get over the shock of turning round this morning and discovering Race Williams in the same room. Of all the cruel blows fate could have inflicted upon her! She felt a renewal of her tension as the subject of her thoughts came in and put his empty mug by the sink, his eyes widening fractionally as he watched her.

'Very domesticated—it suits you,' he added unexpectedly, watching her with narrowed eyes. 'Why get so uptight about your height?' he asked softly, startling her, her expression betraying her before she could conceal her reaction. 'Is that what makes you so aggressive?' he asked, still watching her. 'Perhaps it's time that someone taught you that even Amazons are still women?'

'And you're just the man to do it, I suppose,' Heather retaliated angrily. 'Does it never occur to you that a woman might just be sufficient unto herself; that she might not need a man to show her how to be female?'

'Never,' Race told her arrogantly. 'And don't you start telling me that's how you feel. You might not want to admit it, even to yourself, but you aren't immune to sexual desire, Heather.' He moved, too quickly for her to avoid him, his arms coming round her from behind, imprisoning her, his hand resting just below her breast, monitoring the hurried thud of her heart.

'Let go of me!'

She felt the tension in his body. 'Only when I'm good and ready,' he told her thickly. 'Why do you keep on rejecting me? I know you aren't indifferent to me.'

She wasn't. Her body was acutely conscious of his

proximity, of the warmth and strength of him beneath the covering of his clothes. Her heart was racing against his hand and she felt herself drowning in her need to submit to the hypnotic tide of sensuality emanating from him. But she mustn't give in to it. To him she was just a momentary diversion. Someone who had strayed into his life and made the mistake of challenging him. That was what this was all about. Her taunts had stung and he was determined to make her pay for them.

His hands moved upwards, exploring the shape of her breasts, and she had to fight not to react; to control her breathing so that it wouldn't betray her torment. He wasn't just touching her, he was using every ounce of willpower he possessed to dominate, to subdue her.

'You want me, Heather.' He murmured the word against her ear, tracing its delicate shape with his tongue. He had deliberately tricked her into coming up here, but even knowing that she felt herself weakening, giving up to the golden haze of pleasure enveloping her. 'Stop fighting me,' he warned her, and then he was turning her in his arms, his hands sliding down to her waist, holding her against him, his mouth hard and determined on hers, while her body melted against him so completely that her mind reeled in horror.

And Race knew exactly what he was doing to her. The small growl of satisfaction she heard deep in his throat was one of pure male victory, the sweep of his hands against her body so openly possessive that her mind cringed. And then when she had least expected it she was free, her body trembling with reaction, her eyes unknowingly shadowed.

'When I take you to my bed I want you there willingly, wanting the feel of my body against you, as much as I need to feel yours against me,' he told her, answering her unvoiced question. 'I want total capitulation, Heather,' he told her softly, 'nothing else will do.'

And he had trapped her here with that in mind. He would play on her emotions, on her body, until he had reduced her to mindless subjugation, but she would rather die first. Hadn't she learned years ago the folly of giving herself completely to any man, the pain that would automatically follow?

'I want to possess you body and soul,' Race told her thickly, 'and I will do, Heather, I will.'

Just for a moment she saw the man behind the cool, mocking façade and her heart lodged momentarily in her throat, her body responding against her will to the sexual need in his voice, her pulses racing at the primitive explicitness he had expressed.

It was a full five minutes before she could feel calm enough to return to the work she had spread out on the table. Somehow the lives of her characters felt dull and flat, and she stared at her typed notes, forcing her mind to concentrate, reminding herself that until Race came into her life this book had been one of the most important things in it. He overpowered and dominated her, and he frightened her because of the responses he elicited from her. It would be fatally easy to give in, to let herself drown in the floodtide of desire he sparked off inside her, to give herself body and soul into his keeping, letting him direct the course of her life, giving herself completely to him as she knew now he wanted her to; and the knowledge shook her, frightening her because it was so illogical and dangerous.

If she gave in she would eventually have to come to terms with losing him, with the knowledge that he had taken what he wanted and no longer desired her, she had seen it happen to so many other girls, she knew what men were like once their desire was satiated.

She must be mad to even contemplate giving in to him! She had seen the desire blazing in his eyes the first time they met, and despised him for it, or so she had told herself at the time, thinking she could use it as she had used other men, to pay for Brad's deception, but Race had outmanoeuvred her and now she was trapped in this cottage with him, while he stalked her, waiting ... waiting ... with all the patience of a jungle predator waiting to pounce at the first sign of weakness.

Eventually she managed to start work on her book, slowly and painfully at first, until her nerves relaxed, lulled by the sounds of activity from the other room, the clatter of the typewriter interspersed occasionally by some muttered comment from Race, bearing out his earlier claim that when he worked he was totally absorbed in what he was doing. She herself found it much harder, but gradually the old magic started to work, the lives of her characters started to exert their old spell on her, and she was genuinely startled when Race's shadow fell across her notebook, his fingers pushing through his hair as he studied what she was doing.

She covered the book instantly, suddenly protective of her work, not wanting him to see and criticise, but to her surprise he did neither, simply perching on the edge of the table, studying her shuttered mutinous face for a while before saying, 'Terry tells me that you started to write when you were in your teens—like me. My mother wanted me to become a doctor. She was very disappointed when I joined our local paper as a reporter, but it was what I'd always wanted to do.' His mother? Strange he should mention her and not his father!

'But you left Fleet Street?' Heather was interested in spite of herself, consumed by a sudden craving to discover as much about him as she could.

'Yes, because I'd gone as far as I could go. I'd lost the gut-gripping excitement, the sheer thrill of what I was doing, and I knew the time had come to stop. I'd had enough of foreign lands, political quarrels, wars, dying and maimed children, so I stopped.'

'And started to write?'

'And started to write,' he agreed, 'among other things. And that's something that still hasn't lost its appeal. What do you fancy for lunch?'

It was so mundane a question that Heather almost laughed. They could have been any married couple working comfortably together, sharing. . . . She fought back the thought, worried that she should ever have had it, frowning. 'Is an omelette okay?'

'Yes . . . yes, fine.' She tried not to watch him and lost the battle, as he moved round the kitchen, obviously quite at home, quick and efficient as he prepared their meal. 'It's getting colder,' he told her, as he handed her a warmed plate with a fluffy light omelette on it. 'I don't know whether that's because the temperature is dropping, or because there's something wrong with the heating. I'd better go out and have another look at the generator after lunch.' Just as he finished speaking the lights flickered again, suddenly going out.

'Damn!' Race swore feelingly. 'Looks like the generator's gone. Hang on.' He got up and went to the kitchen cupboards, producing two old-fashioned oil lamps. 'Roy MacNeil loaned me these last year—I'll see if I can get them working.'

Without the illumination of the electric lights, the cottage was quite dark, and suddenly colder. Heather realised, shivering, despite her shirt and thick jumper, the sudden reality of just how cold it would be without the heating striking through her.

'I'll do that,' she offered. 'I do know how, my aunt and uncle live in a small village and keep some for emergencies. You could go and see if you can get the generator working again.'

'Thanks!' Race released the lamps to her without any demur, and Heather bent over them, not looking as he walked towards the door. He was gone over fifteen minutes, returning with his arms full of logs, and Heather's heart sank when she realised what they meant. She had managed to light the lamps without too much trouble and their soft glow illuminated the kitchen.

'It's no go with the generator,' Race told her. 'I'll go back and get the gaz for the cooker, and bring in some more logs. Can you manage to get the fire going? Strange, I hadn't thought of you as being so practical.'

'Because I'm a model my head must be stuffed with cotton wool, is that it?' Heather taunted. 'I didn't think you were so predictable.'

He laughed at her sardonic comment, watching her twist up paper for the fire. 'There's obviously much more to you than a pretty face and a sexy body,' he agreed. 'Tell me more about your family. Have you any brothers and sisters?'

So there were some things Jennifer hadn't told him. 'No,' she told him curtly, refusing to enlarge on her denial. 'Hadn't you better go and get that gaz?'

She had the fire well alight by the time he had finished fitting the gaz cyclinder to the cooker, giving the mechanism a final turn before testing it. A reassuring jet of flame burned on the ring, and he grunted his satisfaction before joining her in front of the fire. 'Full marks,' he approved, watching her, bending towards her and grasping her chin before she could move out of the way, and then licking his finger and rubbing it across the bridge of her nose, the oddly intimate gesture stifling her breath in her throat. 'You've got a dirty mark on your face,' he told her. 'Why don't you like talking about yourself?'

Why, oh, why did she always fall into the trap, relaxing one moment and then feeling her stomach plunge as though she were shooting up in a high-speed lift the next, when he caught her off guard with an unexpected question?

'What makes you think I don't?' she countered, biting her lip when he murmured, 'Answering a question with another question is highly defensive. Why are you always so anxious to keep the world at bay? People normally only do that when they've been badly hurt. Is that it, Heather,' he asked her smokily, 'is that what it's all about? Have you been hurt?'

'It's none of your damned business!' she managed to get furiously. Who the hell did he think he was? Some sort of amateur Freud?

'When did it happen?' he pressed, ignoring her obvious reluctance to talk. 'Tell me about it.'

'Why? So that you can gloat? So that you can throw it in my face? All right, I will tell you,' she cried recklessly. 'Yes, I was hurt ... and it was all my own stupid fault, because I was crazy enough to believe someone might actually love me. Me! The girl every boy loved to make fun of!

'Are you happy now?' she asked in a high, tense voice. 'Have you heard what you wanted to hear? Is that clever brain of yours working overtime on how you can turn it to your advantage? Well, you can't,' she told him grittily. 'What I learned then inoculated me for all time against men like you. . . .'

'And no one's going to get the chance to hurt you

again?' Race said softly. 'But I don't want to hurt you, Heather. I just want to make love to you.'

Didn't he know that it was the same thing? That by making her love him he would ultimately hurt her when he eventually rejected her? Making her love him? Heather shivered. He hadn't mentioned love, he had simply talked about possession of her body. What was the matter with her?

'What about your parents?' he asked conversationally. 'Where do they live?'

'Nowhere, they're dead,' she told him tonelessly. 'Jennifer's parents brought me up. Anything else you want to know, like are all my teeth my own?'

'Are they?' he countered tauntingly. 'You're as prickly as a hedgehog, reluctant to give even the slightest bit of yourself away, hoarding everything away like a miser.'

'And you're trying to dissect me to discover what makes me tick,' Heather retorted, 'hoping that I'll lower my guard and. . . .'

'And what? Remember that you're a woman? The fire seems to have caught properly now,' he told her, standing up so suddenly that her eyes travelled automatically along the length of his legs, the fabric of his cords stretched tight over taut muscles, his eyes looking down into hers registering the emotions revealed in them, his mouth a lazy smile of satisfaction as he watched her.

It was cold in the kitchen without the central heating, and during the afternoon when Race suggested that they could share the table in the living room to work on, Heather was too chilled to demur. He helped her carry her work through, asking her several questions about what she was doing, both intelligent and interested. In other circumstances, without the sexual overtones and implications implicit in their relationship, without her fear and hatred of his sex, they could have been friends. She admired his work and sensed that he would help her with hers if she were to ask, but she was reluctant to do so, to take anything from him in case he turned round and demanded payment. She was too proud to take anything she was not prepared to pay for, especially when she knew the coin he would demand.

Just after six he leaned back in his chair and stretched, the movement pulling the wool fabric of his shirt taut across his chest, bones cracking in his fingers. He was superbly fit, and Heather wondered what sports he indulged in to keep that way. There wasn't an ounce of superfluous fat on his body, and yet neither was it in the slightest musclebound. His nails were cut short, clean and well cared for, his hair shiny with health and vitality, his body reminding her of a lean, coiled animal in the peak of physical condition.

'What time's dinner?'

Heather glanced at her watch. 'Any time you're ready. Are you hungry?'

'Now there's a leading question.' She blushed and hated herself for doing so as he laughed and stood up, tensing when his hands descended on her shoulders. 'Relax, you're as tense as a piece of fine-drawn wire. These muscles,' he pressed her shoulders, 'can't you feel the tension in them?'

She could, and it was useless protesting to him that until he touched her she had been perfectly relaxed. She could feel his fingers moving against the back of her neck stroking and coaxing locked muscles pushing aside her hair and sliding down inside her jumper as he massaged her shoulders. She wanted to tell him to stop, but somehow the words wouldn't come, as heat stroked through her body from the fingertips kneading her flesh. She closed her eyes, telling herself that she might as well try and relax, unaware of the shaken breath she expelled, unaware of anything but the sensual stroke of Race's hands, until suddenly they were withdrawn, his lips touching the back of her neck briefly before he straightened to say, 'That's better, you seem much more relaxed now. It's typing that does it.'

'Thanks very much.' How tight and cold her voice sounded. She could only pray that he hadn't guessed how much his touch had affected her.

'My pleasure. If you're very good I'll teach you how to give a body massage—it's very therapeutic.'

She could see the amusement glinting in his eyes and knew that she had coloured, wild images of her hands against his body flooding through her mind, appalling her with their intimacy.

It was all part of a deliberately planned campaign, she thought bitterly when her colour had died down. Race was using her own vulnerability as a weapon against her, constantly making her aware of him, tightening the coil of fear cum anticipation within her and then releasing it, each time tightening it a little further. She ignored him as she prepared their dinner. The casserole was cooked and she added more vegetables, thickening the stew slightly, clearing her work away so that she could lay the table. Race had gone upstairs, and she could hear the sound of running water. He was probably having a shower, and she frowned wondering whether the fire heated any hot water. She would have to ask him when he came down.

He arrived just as she was about to serve the meal, his cords and shirt exchanged for narrow black pants and a matching shirt, open at the front, moisture still glinting on the fine hairs darkening his chest. When he saw her eyes widen he said solemnly, 'One most always observes the niceties of life. Why don't you join me? Something like that black dress you wore at the studio would be very nice.'

Heather wanted to hit him for the look in his eyes. How was it possible for one man to arouse so many varied and contrasting emotions inside her? One part of her yearned to march upstairs and refute his implied allegation that she looked unfeminine by putting on the sexiest thing she could find, the other wanted to show him exactly how little his opinion mattered by staying exactly as she was. In the end she simply told him that she felt too cold to change, which wasn't far from the truth. He must be much hardier than she was, because he was wearing far less and looked perfectly at ease whereas her feet and legs were already quite cold.

To her relief Race told her that the fire did heat the water. She would have a hot bath before going to bed, she decided as he said approvingly that she was a very good cook. The only problem was, where was she going to sleep? She looked at the small settee, which was nowhere near long enough to accommodate her, but which would have to do. She would have to pile her coat on top of it to keep her warm unless she could find any more bedclothes, but at least she would have the comfort of the fire. Deliberately she looked away, not wanting Race to guess what she was thinking. He wouldn't force her, he had said. Well, time would tell, but she was banking on him having told the truth.

A little to her surprise he insisted on helping her with the washing up, and when it was finished he went to sit by the fire, selecting a book from the shelves and settling down to read it. How long did he intend to stay there? Heather wondered. She could hardly go to bed until he left.

She went upstairs to see if she could find any bedclothes, and managed to unearth a couple of thin blankets from the airing cupboard in the bathroom. They were better than nothing and would have to do. She daren't attempt to take the duvet, because she was sure Race would re-possess it.

When she went back downstairs he was still engrossed in his book, and she went into the kitchen intending to make them both a drink, alarmed to discover how much colder it was. She had brought a battery radio with her and she switched it on, waiting to hear a weather forecast. It hadn't stopped snowing all day, the wind still keened outside. She knew it was impossible for her to leave.

'Come and sit down. I'm not going to pounce on you and devour you, you know.'

Once again he had caught her off guard, and weakly she let him finish making the coffee and carry it through into the living room. 'You intrigue me,' he told her when they were sitting down. 'Such a mass of contradictions. . . .'

'And because I intrigue you, you want me?' Heather said tightly, suddenly angered by the way he was looking at her, slowly undressing her as he had done once before, caressing her so blatantly that she only had to close her eyes to feel his hands against her body.

'That and . . . other reasons,' Race admitted, smiling. 'At least I'm honest,' he told her. 'You want me too, but you won't admit it. I could take you to bed now and make you admit it, but I don't want that, Heather.'

'No, you want total victory,' she said bitterly, 'total capitulation. . . .'

'Yes,' he agreed softly, no longer smiling. 'That's what I want, and that's what I mean to have.'

CHAPTER FIVE

IT was no good—no matter which way she turned, she was still frozen, Heather thought tiredly, her mind and body craving sleep, but too cold for her to relax her hold on consciousness, too aware of Race, no doubt sleeping comfortably in the bedroom above her. She tried not to think about him, but it was impossible; he filled her mind as no man had done since Brad, and part of her ached to be with him right now. The knowledge shocked her and she tried to dismiss it, to push it out of her mind, telling herself that she was simply reacting to the psychological war he was waging on her to wear down her resistance.

Her feet were almost numb, aching with cold. Perhaps a hot drink would warm her up a bit. Shivering, Heather pushed back the covers and huddled deeper into the old dressing gown she had brought with her, camel-haired and shabby, but tonight she was grateful for its comfort.

The flagged kitchen floor felt icy beneath her feet, her breath white in the coldness. In the living room at least there was the heat of the banked-down fire, although it was not enough to remove the ice from her veins. She filled the kettle, reaching for a mug, shivering so badly that she knocked it to the floor, fortunately without breaking it. She was just waiting for the kettle to come to the boil when she heard footsteps behind her, and tensed automatically. Race! Why had he come downstairs?

'What was all that crashing about?' he demanded, coming over to her. He was wearing the same robe he had worn that morning, and Heather hastily averted her eyes from the deep triangle of tanned flesh and dark hair exposed.

'I . . . I was cold,' she admitted, 'and thought I'd make myself a drink.'

'Cold?' He reached out and touched her hand before she could withdraw, cursing fluently as he felt the icy chill of her skin. 'Cold? You're frozen. Enough is enough, Heather,' he told her authoritatively. 'Protest as much as you like, but I'm not leaving you down here to freeze. You're coming back to bed—with me.'

She did protest, covering the surge of sensation exploding inside her with only half assumed anger.

'Look, if it makes you feel any better, I've already told you, I've no intention of forcing you to submit to me. When I take you, it's going to be because we both want it. Quite frankly, right now you're the one who's got her mind on sex, not me—all I'm thinking about is the possibility of coming downstairs tomorrow morning and finding you suffering from hypothermia. You aren't used to these conditions. I bet it's years since you lived anywhere that isn't centrally heated?'

Heather couldn't deny his sardonic comment, and suddenly she ached to be warm again, too much to offer any substantial protest when Race swung her off her feet and carried her towards the door. Her hands went to his shoulders automatically to steady herself, her breath held, fearing that he would drop her—after all, she was no petite five foot nothing, but his breathing barely registered any strain, only a brief, mocking smile acknowledging her alarm and the reasons for it.

'Put your arms round my neck,' he told her calmly. 'I won't drop you—at least, not without some warning.'

The sensation of being held in his arms was a vaguely traumatic one, taking her back to a time when her father had carried her like this, when she had been part of an intimate family unit. Her aunt and uncle loved her, she knew that, but her uncle was small, plump and balding, and when she had gone to them after her parents' death she had been taller than any of her cousins and almost as tall as her uncle. He had never picked her up, he wasn't that kind of man, and the knowledge of how much she had missed that essential physical contact swept over her. Because she was tall she had been expected to stand alone, and not even to herself had she admitted her need to be treated occasionally as though she were vulnerable and fragile.

They were at the top of the stairs, Race bending his head as he kicked open the bedroom door. 'Relax,' he told her softly, 'I'm not about to pounce on you.'

He had obviously lit one of the oil lamps when he heard her moving about downstairs and long shadows danced on the ceiling and in the corners of the room. The air was bitterly cold, but the bed, when Race pulled back the duvet and dropped her on to it, still held traces of his body heat, so blissful to her cold limbs that she barely noticed when he extinguished the lamp and got in beside her, the bed depressing under his weight, fear feathering along her spine until she realised he was lying with his back to her, apparently not in the least disturbed by her presence. The minutes ticked by as she tried to relax, willing her tense muscles into submission, wishing she could stop shivering with the cold that seemed to have bitten deep into her bones. She was still wearing her dressing gown, and she curled up inside it, her feet and legs icy, her teeth still chattering. Race seemed to be asleep, warmth radiating from his body, reaching out to envelop and draw her closer, compelling her to inch towards him with the same primaeval need that draws moths to flutter round a flame.

At one point during the night Heather surfaced from a dream in which she had been telling Brad that she knew why he wanted her, to find her face wet with tears, but her body blissfully warm and relaxed, curled against something solid and smooth and so comforting that the misery of her dream evaporated, and she cuddled closer into the womb-like warmth surrounding her with a soft sigh of satisfaction.

Morning! Heather opened her eyes and blinked at the brilliance of the sunlight flooding the room, turning her head towards the window and stiffening as she realised the warm pressure against her body was Race, his arm curled round her waist, holding her against him. She tried to move his arm and wriggle free, but his hand simply lifted and moved up her body, coming to rest possessively against her breast, a sleepy murmur, warning her that he was on the verge of waking up, the pad of his thumb moving drowsily against her nipple, the lazy caress making her bitterly aware of his familiarity with the female form and the fact that he was no stranger to waking up with a woman in his arms. She tried again to wriggle free, tensing as she felt him stir, the pressure of his fingers hardening, seeking the softness of her body beneath her nightdress.

'Mmm, you feel just like a woman should,' she heard Race whisper behind her, his voice lazy with the satisfaction of touching her, his lips warm as they explored the exposed nape of her neck, his free hand pushing aside her hair, his laughter shivering across her skin as he encountered the thick fabric of her dressing gown, his coaxing, 'You know you'd feel much warmer without this,' sending tremors running along her spine, visions of herself naked in his arms making her regret her weakness of the previous night.

Better to have remained cold and safe downstairs,

but it was too late to think of that now. Race was already easing the dressing gown off her shoulders, pinning her arms behind her back as he did so, her scrabbling fingers stilling in shock as they came into contact with the tautly muscled flatness of his stomach.

He laughed again, almost silently, but she could feel his breath shivering across her skin, the fact that she was lying with her back towards him making it far too easy for him to slide the dressing gown from her body without her being able to do a single thing about it, other than kick back at him angrily, twisting and turning as she tried to free the hands he held pinioned behind her back. Her nightdress was an old cotton one, and where he had unfastened the ribbons at the front the upper curves of her breasts were exposed, rising and falling urgently as she tried to fight free of him. Her hands were released and her dressing-gown finally removed in one easy moment, the breath leaving her lungs on a startled gasp as he turned her on to her back, trapping her there with the weight of his thigh, her body registering the nudity of his body as at the same moment she lifted her hands to push him away.

'You said you wouldn't touch me,' she reminded him huskily, knowing that reminding him was her best defence and that she could never overcome him physically.

'Unless you wanted me to,' he agreed.

Heather's eyes smouldered. 'I don't.'

'No?'

Her palms were pressed flat against his chest, the muscles in her arms rigid as she held him off, her eyes furious and bitter as she struggled not to look away from him. With one mercilessly swift movement he pushed her nightdress off her shoulders, completely exposing her breasts. His fingers locked on her wrists, pulling her hands away from his chest, and forcing them back down to her side.

When he bent slowly towards her Heather felt as though her breath were suspended somewhere in her throat. Her heart started to beat with slow, heavy, choking thuds, her eyes locked on Race's until he bent his head to her breasts. Something deep inside her longed to scream out to him to stop, urging her to give way to admit defeat, but stubbornly she refused, telling herself that she would not show her fear, that she would withstand him no matter what she felt inside. She closed her eyes, willing herself not to react, digging her fingers into the mattress as she anticipated the touch of his mouth against her skin. Despite the cold, perspiration broke out on her forehead, her mouth was dry, her body shaking inwardly as she waited . . . and waited . . . and then at last opened her eyes to find Race watching her mockingly.

'Now tell me again you don't want me, Heather,' he told her, watching her as her eyes slid from his to the aroused and tormented peaks of her breasts, swollen and aching in anticipation of his touch.

Humiliation washed over her, drowning out every other feeling. She gave a small, inarticulate cry, hating him for seeing her like this, for making her feel like this, then she wrenched her arms away, curling her body into a small ball, as she tried to hide herself from him.

'Are you happy now?' she demanded in a thick choked voice. 'Now that you've won, that. . . .'

'Heather.' She felt his hands on her shoulders and stiffened in rejection. 'Heather, we aren't at war, you know. I don't feel ashamed of wanting you and there's no reason why you should feel ashamed of wanting me. Have you any idea what it does to me to know

you want me and that you'll do anything to deny that
want? It isn't exactly ego-building,' he assured her
dryly. 'You were crying in your sleep last night,' he
told her huskily, 'because someone a long time ago
hurt you, but when I took you in my arms you
stopped crying and you cuddled up against me as
trustingly as a child. I damn near woke you up and
took you then,' he told her, his voice suddenly
hoarsely uneven.

'Have you any idea of what you do to me?' he
demanded savagely. 'What you experienced just now
is only a thousandth of it, and the insane thing is that
there's no need for either of us to feel like that. We
want each other, Heather, our bodies are crying out
for one another, you can make my body react just as
hungrily simply by looking at me.' He turned her over
again and Heather felt herself quiver in fear and
longing as he looked at her, uncrossing the arms she
had folded over her breasts, his breathing suddenly
unsteady.

An inarticulate murmur strangled in his throat, his
mouth hotly possessive against her breast, and a fierce
current of pleasure ran through her body like jagged
lightning from the hard centre of her breast. Race
muttered something against her skin, breathing
heavily, his heart thudding unsteadily as he released
her nipple to circle it with his tongue, the flood of
desire rising swiftly inside her making her arch and
murmur his name, her fingers biting into his
shoulders, her body abandoning her to a sea of sensual
pleasure.

'Tell me ... tell me ... you want me. ...' Race
interspersed the demand with tormenting caresses,
melting her body, dissolving it until there was nothing
but the raging need he was building inside her, and
her feverish, 'Race ... please. .. !' brought his mouth

down on hers with a hunger that matched her own, fanning the mingled flames of anger and need that burned through her, passion a dark underground river that possessed her just as surely as Race meant to.

'I want you.' Even his heart seemed to thud out the words, his mouth hot against her skin exploring it hungrily, trapping the pulse thudding at the base of her throat, the grey glitter of his eyes as they swept over her body making her shiver uncontrollably. 'I want you, Heather,' he told her thickly, 'all of you, body, mind and soul—I want to possess you: I want you to give yourself to me in a way you've never given yourself to anyone else.'

His intensity half frightened and half excited her. She could feel the clamorous response of her blood to the thickly uttered words, the glinting absorption in his eyes as they feasted on her body. 'I wanted you the first time I saw you—at a party. You didn't notice me. You were with someone else. I wanted to kill him, to tear him apart limb by limb, and then make love to you while the blood lust still possessed my body. That's how passion is, Heather; it isn't neat and clean and antiseptic, it's wanting mingled with anger and rage, resentment at the wanting and a fierce elemental hunger that has to be satisfied. That's how I want you, Heather. . . . That's how I want you to want me, so much that you'll go mindless with the intensity of it, that you'll forget every other man you've ever known. Kiss me,' he ordered, his voice thick with emotion, and slow. 'Kiss me, Heather. . . .'

She obeyed him almost blindly, still trying to assimilate the meaning of his words, still trying to come to terms with her own reactions to them, that he would want her so much and without emotion astounded her. The feelings he had described were those of an obsession, his need to possess her obsessive

in its intensity. When he talked to her she had had
vivid images of the two of them together, their
lovemaking feverishly violent and savagely necessary,
and they shook her because she had never felt like
that, never even thought of wanting that kind of sexual
excitement.

But he had made her want it, made her ache to
touch him, to caress and arouse him, to give herself
completely to him . . . but that wasn't wanting. That
was love! She stilled, closing her eyes, trying to
overcome the sick shaky sensation coiling inside her
but knowing it was true. She did love him. That first
time she had seen him she had reacted to him, and
because she resented that reaction she had called it
dislike. And then that time at his house, her body had
known then what her mind refused to admit. She had
fallen in love with him at first sight like an adolescent.
And he wanted her.

But what was 'wanting'? Only an appetite that once
satiated, was gone. The sudden realisation of what her
life would be without him appalled her. How could
this have happened to her? She didn't know, she only
knew that it had, and all at once she knew she had to
get away from Race, it was imperative that she did.
She couldn't stay and hide from him how she felt, and
he, male-like, would revel in the discovery of how she
felt about him. She had no illusions about that. He
might not love her, but her love for him would feed
his ego, and he would take advantage of it, just as his
body would delight in forcing her submission no
matter how often he told her he wanted her to come to
him willingly. Some instinct she hadn't known she had
told her that he would find pleasure in letting her defy
him, only to reduce her to hungry need in his arms.

He hadn't lied when he said he resented wanting
her. She could feel that resentment in the way he

touched her, see in the glitter of his eyes, and it was because of that resentment, to appease it that he would stop at nothing.

His hands stroked compulsively over her body, touching and learning the texture of her skin, registering the response she couldn't hide from him, satisfaction gleaming in the depths of his eyes, his voice hoarse with urgency as need broke through the control he was exercising, his heart thudding unevenly against her as he groaned her name, parting her thighs with his knee, the throbbing arousal of his body communicated intimately to hers, his mouth hot and possessive as it closed over hers, making her moan deep in her throat and arch instinctively beneath him, welcoming the heat of his body against her.

'Heather, touch me. Pleasure me.' The huskily muttered command shivered over her skin, eliciting an age-old wanton need to respond, and her fingertips pressed feverishly against his shoulders, exploring the bones and muscle, her lips arching to follow the same path, before she realised the ultimate conclusion to which her actions would lead.

Suddenly angry with herself and him, Heather pulled back. Twenty-four hours, that was all it had taken Race to persuade her into his bed, and she, poor fool that she was, had let him.

She looked up into his face, knowing he could not have mistaken her withdrawal. His eyes were brilliant with baffled fury and frustration, his thoughts for once completely unguarded. 'I don't think I believe this,' Heather heard him say tensely. 'I told you before, I won't force you, Heather, but damn you for a hypocrite—and worse—if you stop me now,' he added thickly. 'You know you want me as much as I want you.'

'I thought I did,' Heather admitted slowly. She

must be very careful what she said now. She had no intention of allowing him to guess how she felt about him; if she did he would simply use the information against her, forcing her submission through her love, although, of course, he would cloak it in other words, say that she gave herself 'willingly'. But she had no intention of letting him make love to her. To do so would be to sacrifice the rules by which she lived her life, to destroy her own self-respect.

'I thought I did,' she repeated, taking a deep breath and praying that what she was going to say would have the desired effect, 'but I'm afraid mere sexual desire isn't enough, Race. You said you wouldn't force me,' she reminded him, holding his eyes, 'and I intend to hold you to that.'

It was almost more than she could bear to endure the look of bitter frustration combined with cold contempt that she could see in his eyes. 'Damn you!' He swore softly, adding something else under his breath which she barely caught, but which brought a dull tide of colour to her skin.

'Do you play this game with all your men?' he demanded as he released her, 'wind them up until they're begging you, and then turn them down cold? What you're doing is dangerous, Heather. It's tantamount to asking to be raped,' he told her contemptuously, only the ragged sound of his breathing betraying the fact that he wasn't fully in control. 'Is that what you like? To drive a man so far that he can't damn well stop himself from taking you? Does that give you a thrill of power, to watch the poor devil writhing in abject self-contempt whichever path he chooses? Well, that's not going to happen to me. Perhaps I'm not as gentlemanly as all your other men either, because it's going to give me a great deal of satisfaction to know that you're damn near aching for satisfaction as much as I am myself. A satisfaction I wouldn't give you now if you went down on your knees and begged me for it,' he finished crudely.

Heather heard the door close behind him and guessed he had gone into the bathroom. She knew now that he was gone that she ought to get up and get dressed and that staying here in bed, wrapped in the sheet that still smelled tormentingly of his body, was tantamount to begging him, but her mind felt too bruised for her to do anything else. She had experienced male frustration-orientated anger before, but never to such an extent, never quite so painfully.

Because she loved him, she acknowledged with painful inner honesty. Because she loved him she had wanted to give herself to him, had wanted to know the fevered pleasure of his possession. He was right, her body did still ache for him. She touched her pale skin curiously, still bemused by the sensations she had experienced under his hands, her nipples tingling into aroused hardness as she remembered how he had. . . .

Quickly she left the bed, getting clean clothes from her case, promising herself a shower later when Race was downstairs.

The kitchen felt freezing cold, the fire still barely burning in the living-room. She fed it with logs, trying not to shiver as she went into the kitchen and turned on the tap, praying that the pipes had not frozen during the night. They had been lucky, and the water flowed freely, icy cold against her fingers, her breath white plumes in the cold air. Outside the sun was shining brilliantly, but it held no warmth, rather it was the icy dazzle of a diamond reflecting the light, the glare bouncing off the snow, half blinding her as she searched the now peaceful landscape.

The kettle was boiling when she felt rather than heard Race walk into the room. She didn't turn round, her legs suddenly weak as she wondered how on earth she was going to face him. It helped to know that he was still probably too angry to judge her feelings with any accuracy, and besides, she was the only one who knew that the intimacies they had just shared, she had shared with no one else. Not even Brad had touched her or aroused her like that. But then Brad had never truly wanted her, not in the way that Race did.

Heather felt a quiver run through her body, a yearning need to tell him that she had changed her mind, to feel the hot urgency of his body against hers as she had done earlier. Her nails were gripping into her palms when she turned round, her voice husky and unsteady as she asked if he wanted a cup of coffee. 'I think it's my turn to make the breakfast,' she told him, striving to enforce some normality between them, her pale skin flushing when she saw the sardonic twist of his mouth, the cold contempt in the eyes that stripped her ruthlessly of every last defence, his voice ice-cold as he drawled.

'What game are you playing now, Heather? Showing me how "civilised" you can be? Well, I can tell you that right at this moment I don't feel one damned bit civilised. In fact,' he added still pinning her where she stood with the cold ferocity of his gaze, 'if it wasn't for the fact that I value my self-respect, I'd take you here and now, and make you cry out with the same ache that's tearing at my guts. But it isn't over between us,' he told her softly. 'Look out of that window. See that sunshine? That means it's freezing, and it will probably continue to freeze tonight, which means that even on the very best estimate, even if we don't get any more snow, you and I are trapped here for at least two or three more days. Before we leave here you'll be begging me to take you back to my bed and finish what we started this morning. Begging me,' he reiterated softly, infusing the words with a menace that made them both a vow and a threat.

'I don't see why you should bother,' Heather managed, forcing her features to assume her cool modelling mask, the impenetrable mask behind which she hid from the world. 'Unless you enjoy rape.'

'You can't get out of it that way,' he told her, shaking his head, 'and it won't be rape. No, Heather, if you must put a name to it, call it a blow dealt on behalf of all mankind, or at least all those poor unfortunate specimens of it who have crossed your path. I've been blind. I thought of a hundred different reasons for your coldness, but none of them came anyway near to the truth. You're a tease, Heather, and that's putting it politely. Perhaps it's time, for your own good, that you were taught how very painful that can be.'

His control and determination were formidable weapons, Heather acknowledged, both seemingly indestructible. Views that were reinforced time and time again during the next two days when the freeze continued, and she was tortured by every Machiavellian method of making her aware of him and undermining her self-control that he would think of, and none of them so obvious that she could take him to task.

The little things, like leaning over her as he studied her work, were nothing, taken on their own, but each time her body was made physically aware of him, of the sight and smell of him, until her nerves were tightening in apprehension every time he came within a yard of her. He hadn't suggested she share his bed again. In fact he had unearthed a padded sleeping-bag which she now slept in downstairs. This morning he had come downstairs wearing only jeans and had proceeded to wash at the kitchen sink, claiming that

the kitchen was warmer than the bathroom, and
although she had tried hard not to look at him, time
and time again her eyes had been drawn to the
muscled sleekness of his back, brown from constant
exposure to the sun, as though he was in the habit of
spending many months a year abroad. Her imagination
tortured her with brief, fleeting images of his body, of
him, lounging indolently on some beach, very
probably with a beautiful woman.

Of the two of them, she knew who had accomplished
the most work—and it wasn't her. Oh, she pretended
to work all right, forcing herself to study the books she
had brought with her, but all the time acutely
conscious of Race working on the other side of the
table, his concentration a true and patently deep one.
She knew he cared nothing for her as a person. He
wanted her physically and his pride was wounded
because she had withstood him; there were a hundred
or more reasons why she should keep him at bay, and
she was intelligent enough to know them all. So why
did she lie awake at night thinking of him, wishing she
was sharing the large double bed with him, wishing
that lean, powerful male body was her only covering?

Desire, without love, was something she didn't want
to experience, but Race exerted a magnetic pull on her
senses which was fed by her love for him, and she was
bitterly afraid that with every day that passed her
ability to hold him at bay was lessening. She tried to
concentrate on her writing, knowing it was impossible
when a mediaeval de Travers who had defied his
family to fight alongside Richard III took on all Race's
physical attributes, and the girl he loved, a cousin who
Heather had intended would reject him in favour of a
staunchly Lancastrian neighbour, gave herself to him
with an intensity of passion that startled Heather when
she eventually read what she had written.

She was no fool, and her mouth compressed a little grimly when she had finished with the typewritten sheets. What she had written about there were her own feelings, her own desires, and they had been powerful enough to change the course of her book. Even so, she couldn't bring herself to change what she had written.

She glanced across at Race, the dark head bent over some papers of his own, his involvement in what he was reading total. When he wasn't deliberately making her aware of him, he ignored her completely, a subtle form of torture that Heather was intelligent enough to recognise, but not emotionally strong enough to withstand. She glanced out of the window. After brilliant sunshine for almost two days, the sky was starting to cloud again. A thaw had been forecast, but Race had mocked her when he heard it, warning her that they were high up enough not to be affected by it.

How much longer would her self-control last? She knew exactly by what degree, daily, her heartbeat accelerated when Race tormented her by stripping in front of her while he washed at the sink, a ploy which she knew to be completely deliberate, and the effectiveness of which she refused to acknowledge by leaving the room, maintaining a pretence of indifference to his body which she was far from feeling. That and a dozen or so gestures similarly designed to make her aware of him were fast undermining her control, and Race, she was sure, knew it.

CHAPTER SIX

'WE'RE out of logs, I'd better go and get some more.'

The laconic comment was no different from the half a dozen or so others Race had addressed to Heather during the last couple of days. His glance encompassed her body, clad in the protection of socks, jeans and a thick woollen jumper worn over a much finer under-one, as he got up, and added, 'I must say I'd welcome a thaw, it will be nice to get back to civilisation, to see a woman who acts like a woman.'

His comment was too acutely perceptive, but Heather remained unruffled. She had plenty of pretty and attractive clothes with her that she could have worn and which would have kept her equally warm, but her inner defence mechanism had urged her to choose the least feminine things in her wardrobe, as though by muffling herself up and distorting the shape of her body she could hold Race at bay more easily.

It wasn't the first time he had been out to get more logs, and Heather wasn't too disturbed when fifteen minutes slipped by without him returning. It was her day to prepare lunch and she had made a pie from some tinned meat, adding her own pastry; a little stodgy perhaps, she thought, pulling a slight face and hoping that she wouldn't have put on too much weight during her enforced stay.

When Race had been gone half an hour she began to worry. She opened the back door, shivering in the icy wind that lashed against the cottage, frowning over the footprints that led away from the house in the direction of the lane. Fear, as cold and icy as the wind, clutched at her heart. Had Race gone and left her? Blind panic assailed her, overriding every tenet of logic, her mind unable to cope with anything other than the evidence of those footprints leading away from the house and Race's patent absence.

Perhaps he had got tired of playing games with her, of tormenting her, and perhaps he was yearning, as he had said this morning, for other and more congenial female companionship? Did he intend to leave her here? Was this another part of her punishment?

Shivering with cold and reaction, she closed the kitchen door, leaning tiredly against it. She would give him another fifteen minutes and if he hadn't returned at the end of that time she would. . . . She would go after him, she decided grimly. If he could make it to the village then so could she. She would show him that she was just as capable of leaving as he was, that she detested his company as much as he did hers, that he wasn't alone in wanting to escape their enforced intimacy.

Twenty minutes later, clad in her wellington boots, her thick hooded jacket pulled over her jumpers and firmly zipped up, thick mittens covering her hands, Heather stepped outside. It had started to snow again, thick swirling flakes that stuck to her eyelashes and tasted cold on her tongue, but she followed doggedly in Race's footsteps, her breathing growing laboured as the cold bit into her lungs and tore at her skin, the milling flakes, half blinding her as she bent her body against the wind, refusing to give in to the inner voice that urged her to go back to the cottage and warmth.

'Heather!'

The first time she heard her name she thought she was hallucinating, but the second time she stopped, straightening up to discover its source.

'Heather, just what the hell do you think you're

doing?' This time she recognised Race's voice, and the barely suppressed anger it contained. He was walking towards her—from the cottage, snowflakes clinging to his shoulders and chest.

'Surely you're not that much of a coward? Or is death really preferable to me?'

'Oh, Race!' Heather barely registered his taunting comment. She covered the short distance between them, flinging herself against his body, wrapping her arms round him in her relief to see him, sobbing his name between shaken breaths. 'I thought you'd left me,' she told him huskily. 'I saw your footprints, and. . . .'

'I was just seeing how deep the snow was, estimating our chances of getting out,' he told her, but his tone was absent, as though there was something more important on his mind than the possible length of their imprisonment. He was looking at her with an expression in his eyes that made her catch her breath, her lips unknowingly parting in mute invitation, sweetly hot pleasure firing her blood as he pulled off his gloves and unzipped her jacket to slide his hands beneath her jumper and mould her body, her name thickly unfamiliar on his lips as his fingers bit into her shoulders and his mouth touched exploratively against her lips, his eyes glittering darkly between half closed lids as he muttered something explosively under his breath and then possessed her mouth in a kiss that fed the need she had felt building up inside her for days.

She was starving, starving for the touch and warmth of him, for this hungry assault of desire that matched her own need, for the hard pressure of his body against her, and she was drowning, melting fathoms deep in pleasure, when he pulled away, his movements jerky as he closed her jacket, his face grimly shuttered as he turned her round to face the house and said, 'Come on, let's get back before we freeze.'

But she wasn't freezing, Heather thought light-headedly, she was melting, burning up with a need that whispered siren-like for appeasement, urging her to take what was offered and enjoy it. Race might not love her, but he would be an excellent lover. Her body knew it and turned traitor to her mind. The torment of thinking he had gone, of thinking that she had lost him turned the key that locked the door of her self-control, her only barrier against what she felt for him. Now with that standing open she felt feverish with the desire she had striven to keep hidden, her body pulsating with hunger and need.

When they reached the cottage reality intruded, and she kept her face averted from Race's as she stripped off her jacket and boots, knowing that behind her he was doing the same thing.

Two courses were open to her now. She could either pretend that nothing had happened and trust that Race would follow her lead, but if she did that she would have to endure the knowledge that he knew how she had felt, that she had wanted him, but that she had been too cowardly to admit it. The other alternative made her body tingle with fire and apprehension, but what was the point of denying herself?

All right, so he didn't love her, but he wanted her, and with him her body would experience a pleasure she would never find with anyone else. But what about afterwards? What about when he was tired of her, when she was alone. . . .

She would have her memories, she told herself stubbornly, her body playing the devil's advocate, urging her to give in to the wild flood of desire invading her body. This morning she had experienced for one brief hour the agony of losing him. How on earth was she going to cope with hundreds of such hours? Why try to deceive herself that he would not tire of her? She was sexually inexperienced, no match for his expertise, she was a challenge that once conquered would lose appeal, but none of it was strong enough to hold back her physical longing for him.

Thinking he had left her had forced upon her a crisis point, and which road she took from it depended entirely on her. Race hadn't said a word about the kiss they had shared, but she was willing to bet that he knew almost exactly what she had felt, apart from the fact that he did not know that she loved him, and that was only because as far as he was concerned it was an emotion that simply did not exist. He thought she was motivated by desire as he was himself, and wasn't there a certain element of safety in letting him continue to think that? A salve for her pride when eventually he left her.

Without conscious thought the decision had been reached, but to carry it through demanded a resolution she wasn't sure she possessed. Race had eaten the meal she had served, his eyes narrowing over her own untouched plate, his mouth curling slightly as he drawled, 'Not hungry?'

Now was her chance, all she had to say was 'not for food', all she had to do was look at him with the same naked hunger she had once seen in his eyes ... but somehow her nerve failed her and she shook her head, half stumbling as she got up to remove their plates, Race's hands on her waist steadying her, his lips warm against her ear as he murmured, 'Coward. . . .'

He knew! He knew exactly what she was feeling, thinking, and he wasn't going to make it easy for her. She was pretty sure he had told her he would make her beg in a fit of the temper Jennifer told her he possessed, but in the cold light of day enough damage had been done to his pride by her rejection for him to want to make her suffer. But she couldn't ask him to make love to her, she couldn't!

During the afternoon a further thaw was forecast, and when Race went to close the curtains, he told Heather that it was raining.

'We could be out of here by tomorrow,' he added, 'unless it starts to freeze again. You'd better pray that it doesn't, I think,' he added softly, and Heather knew he was aware of how dangerously close to losing her self-control she was.

It was his turn to cook dinner, and when he suggested a small celebration, she looked at him suspiciously. 'We might as well celebrate the commencement of the thaw, although that wasn't exactly what I had in mind when I brought this with me,' he told her wryly, indicating a bottle of champagne.

Her cheeks still flushed by the implication of his words, Heather escaped upstairs. One more night and then she would be free. So why did she feel so depressed?

She already knew the answer. She studied her clothes absently, unaware that she was reaching for the folds of the one dress she had brought with her, 'just in case', until her fingers brushed the soft fabric. In soft wool, the material had a vaguely tartan design in reds and blacks. The dress buttoned down the front, the collar and cuffs white, the collar faintly puritan. Even before she put it on Heather knew she had chosen the road she intended to take, and resolutely she blinded her mind to all the objections it could raise. Why shouldn't she have tonight? Why shouldn't she have the bitter-sweet pleasure of knowing Race's lovemaking?

She dressed carefully, the new underwear Jennifer had bought her, her favourite perfume, sheer silk stockings and careful make-up, all surely ridiculous when one thought of the remoteness and coldness of the cottage, but just for tonight.

On the point of fastening her dress, she changed her mind, quickly unhooking her bra and putting it away. She had always considered her breasts a little too full for her to go bra-less, but tonight there was something about their soft roundness beneath the fine wool that made her fingers tremble over the buttons as she quickly fastened them before she could change her mind.

Going downstairs was one of the hardest things she had ever done. Race looked up just before she reached the bottom, not saying a word, but his eyes registered every detail of her appearance.

'It seems we're celebrating with a vengeance,' he said at last, and Heather was glad the muted glow of the oil lamps hid her flushed cheeks from him.

'Well, it might be our last night,' she told him lightly, 'we'll soon be back in civilisation.'

'If you wouldn't mind keeping an eye on the meal I could make some attempt to do justice to your . . . metamorphosis.'

Heather wondered at the pause before the last word, trying to guess what he was thinking, if he had been deceived by her claim that she had changed simply because it was their last night, or if he had guessed. . . . There was no indication of his feelings to be read in his expression and she nodded mutely, walking into the kitchen to check on the chicken chasseur cooking in the oven.

Race came back just as she was on the verge of succumbing to a fit of nerves. He had changed into dark, well-fitting pants that clung to his hips and stretched tautly over his thighs as he came downstairs. His shirt was a pale blur in the half-light, open slightly at the throat, his lean fingers busily inserting links into his cuff as he came towards her.

He had found a tin of grapefruit which they had for a starter; the wine he had chilled outside the door was clear and refreshing to Heather's palate. She was normally the most moderate of drinkers, but something in the coolly level grey gaze made her drink more quickly than usual. Would he make her speak her need? Could she?

As she sipped her wine she felt her nerves quieting, and she made no demur when Race refilled her glass, watching him with a building core of sensual excitement as he served the chicken. Every movement he made was economical, and intensely male. The pale silk of his shirt tightened over his body as he served her chicken and she was consumed by a longing to reach out and touch him, to place her lips to the exposed column of his throat and let her tongue delicately explore the tanned flesh.

'Is that enough, Heather?' The sound of his voice jerked her out of her daydream, her cheeks flushing hotly as she realised he had witnessed her absorption.

She could barely touch her food, buoyed up with a nervous excitement that fed on the sight of him in front of her just as the wine she was drinking lent her courage.

When they had finished eating she offered to make the coffee. Race wasn't going to make it easy for her, she knew that now. He had poured them both a glass of champagne and he was seated before the fire, leaning back against the settee, legs outthrust in front of him. He wasn't going to make it easy for her at all, but how could she simply ask him to make love to her? She couldn't. But she could show him what she wanted, and hope that his desire for her would do the rest and that he wouldn't demand full payment for earlier rejection.

Her hands were shaking when she carried the coffee through into the living room. She put her own cup down on a small table by the fire and then took Race's cup to him. There was a table on the opposite side of the settee, and he looked up at her through lashes that concealed his expression too well from her as she approached.

'Put it down here for me, would you, Heather?' he said softly, indicating the table.

She could have walked round and put the cup down on the table, but instead she leaned across him, one hand holding the cup, the other bracing herself against the back of the settee. She knew the action deliberately and tantalisingly outlined the rounded curve of her breasts, and was half appalled at the deliberate enticement of her movements. She had never done anything like this before. She knew Race was watching her, his eyes lingering openly on her body, and excitement tingled through her, curling through the pit of her stomach.

'Thanks.' The laconic word crushed her fantasies of being taken in his arms, the blow to her pride shatteringly humiliating, the urge to run away and hide herself from him compellingly urgent, so urgent that she barely realised that he was still talking until his fingers circled her wrist, holding her where she was, his voice softly tormenting as he murmured, 'What's the matter, Heather? Did I do something to offend you? Or was it something I didn't do? It isn't very nice to be rejected, is it, and I take it that's what all this is about?'

When she didn't reply his free hand moved lazily up her body, her muscles tensing in mingled delight and alarm, as it hovered just beneath her breast. Surely he could hear the pounding of her heart? Surely he must know what he was doing to her?

'What am I expected to do?' he continued mockingly. 'This?' His fingers curled round her breast, his thumb probing its softness. 'Or this?' Her heart seemed to lodge somewhere in her throat as he unfastened several of the small buttons and slid his hand inside her dress, the hand that had been imprisoning her wrist releasing it to transfer it to his shoulder, propelling her against him as his tongue sought and found the puckered flesh of her nipple. A whimpered moan burst past her lips. Race released her, pushing her away.

'It hurts like hell to want someone so badly, doesn't it, Heather?' he demanded with soft savagery that told her how much she had underestimated his original anger. 'It tears you up inside to know you're reduced to that wanting. Well, you know what you have to do, I'm not going to make it easy for you.'

'But you want me. . . .' She was barely aware of saying the words, her brain clouded by alcohol and desire.

'Sure I do, enough to be badly tempted to take all that you're offering me so temptingly right now. But I've got to live with myself afterwards. I've already shown you that I want you, now it's your turn to show me.'

'I can't. . . .'

She withdrew from him shakily, shivering slightly, knowing she couldn't do what he demanded.

'Damn you, you can,' he muttered savagely, 'and you will!' Her wrist was grasped again and she was pulled down against him, overbalancing on to his lap, one hard arm trapping her there, while his lips explored the delicate shaping of her ear, teasing it

with his tongue, deliberately arousing her with
delicate kisses that gave so much but no more and
which left her aching for more. His fingers deftly
unfastened the buttons of her dress, pushing it back
off her shoulders until her body was exposed to the
waist, his lips continuing to tease tiny kisses against
her face, refusing to touch her mouth, a violent hunger
raging through her as he continued to torment her.

The silk of his shirt felt damp against her breasts
and suddenly was an intolerable barrier between their
bodies. Barely aware of what she was doing, Heather
tore at the small buttons, pressing her mouth
feverishly against the taut skin of Race's throat when
the last one gave way and she was free to wrap her
arms round his neck, her breasts surging against his
body, aching for the arousing rasp of his body hair
against them, small whimpers of pleasure escaping her
lips as they explored the smooth contours of his skin,
her fingers tensing on the hard muscles of his back,
willing him to respond, to share her need and fuel it.
Couldn't he see that she was telling him without
words how much she needed him? Wasn't it enough
that her body betrayed her with every single action
without her tongue following suit?

Angry now, she wanted to torment him as he was
tormenting her, she wanted to hear him groan her
name against her skin, to feel the tension in his body
she knew was in hers, to push him beyond the
boundaries of his self-control, as he had pushed her.
Her fingertips explored the breadth of his back, her
lips moving against his throat. He had stopped kissing
her and the knowledge acted like a goad. How could
he remain so aloof? She would *make* him respond.

Suddenly heedless of the consequences, her fingers
explored the line of hair arrowing down towards his
waistband, feeling the solid compacting of muscles,

sensing by instinct alone that he was not as indifferent
to her as he pretended. Her palm smoothed lightly
across his chest, registering an unmistakable and
unexpected response, and heat flooded through her
body as she remembered her feverish response when
his tongue touched *her* body. She bent her head,
tracing a line of kisses along his collar bone and then
down, deliberately exploring the unfamiliar shape of
the male nipple beneath her tongue, feeling the sudden
satisfying clench of his muscles, hearing his hoarsely
muttered, 'For God's sake, Heather, tell me you want
me, and stop tormenting us both!'

His susceptibility made it easy for her to murmur
the words against his skin between kisses, feeling his
involuntary response to the touch of her lips, knowing
the initiative was being taken from her, when their
positions were reversed and he was the one to torment
the aching tips of her breasts until she was murmuring
incoherent little pleas which he seemed to have no
difficulty in correctly translating as his teeth tugged
satisfyingly on the swollen flesh, and she arched
blindly towards him, her body gilded rose-gold by the
firelight as she offered herself completely to him and
he held her away, studying her satisfaction and hunger
blended in the hot scrutiny of his eyes as they
surveyed her response to his lovemaking.

'I'm not going to rush this,' he murmured thickly as
he watched her. 'I've waited too damned long for it.'

He touched her hair, cascading down on to her
shoulders, and pulled off her dress, surveying the
delicate bones of her ankles, his glance moving
upwards over her thighs in the pure silk stockings. She
lay motionless beneath his gaze, tensing only when his
fingers travelled up her thigh and pushed aside the
barrier of her French knickers, the kiss he placed there
burning against her skin. Her stockings were removed,

her body trembling beneath the assault of his hands and lips as they caressed the skin they exposed. On Race's face was a look of total concentration; of intensity that told her the extent of his desire. When she lay naked in his arms she felt him expel his breath, her tremulous inclination to hide herself from him prevented as he held her arms at her side and studied her raptly. 'Undress me, Heather,' he commanded unsteadily, 'touch me . . . kiss me. . . .'

He lifted her hands to his body, waiting in tense expectation as she struggled to obey him, trying to ignore the movement of his fingers against the inside of her thigh, sending spirals of pleasure higher and higher inside her until at last he was free of his clothes, and she was free to explore and adore the hard shape of his body, which despite its maleness was as vulnerable to the pangs of desire as hers. She wriggled away from him, from the disturbing contact of his hand against her thigh, stroking her fingers over the lean flatness of his stomach, following the line of dark hair with her tongue, her hands copying the stroke of his along his thighs, until he shuddered and reached for her, imprisoning her against him, caressing her body until he reached the soft, female core of her, making her suck in her breath on a whimper of pleasure that brought a smile to his eyes and an instant physical response from his body as he pulled her tautly into the cradle of his hips, moving urgently against her as her body took brief satisfaction from the contact that somehow wasn't enough.

His lips explored her throat, the small murmured sounds of pleasure he made every time she responded to him finding an echoing response in her. Her hands locked behind his head as he moved languorously down her body, breathing in its warm scents, his lips taking pleasure in the fullness of her breasts.

She cried out in protest as he moved away from her, forbidding her the pleasure of touching him, the warm pressure of his lips against her inner thigh making her want to tense in protest and yet at the same time reluctant to display her naïveté until it was too late to stop his sensuous invasion, his tongue continuing its spiralling investigation of her thigh, moving higher and higher, until she cried out in protest.

His voice hoarse and tight almost unrecognisable, Heather heard him mutter, dragging the breath into his lungs, 'Yes, yes, my gypsy girl, tell me what you want . . . just tell me, Heather,' his tongue continuing its probing until she was gasping his name, writhing in shame tinged pleasure, unable to stop herself from reaching for him, drawing him against her, pressing fevered kisses against his moist skin, her teeth nipping and biting until he covered her mouth with the heat of his, slowly looking at her as she looked back with passion-drugged eyes.

Kneeling astride her, he guided her hands to his body, his voice thick and slurred, his hands on her increasing her own excitement, her body twisting and threshing sensually against them as he held her poised on the threshold of a pleasure she could only anticipitate, making her wait as he moved slowly into her, his hoarse, 'No!' as she tried to move stilling the convulsive restlessness of her body as it tried to match the fierce rhythm of his; his fingers biting into her arms, until he muttered thickly against her throat, 'Now, Heather . . . please, now!' releasing her arms to hold her against him, silencing her with the fierce demand of his mouth. Her body matched him in the elemental, wild storm that rocked them both, pain dimly felt and soon forgotten as pleasure exploded inside her in convulsive waves and Race cried out her name in primaeval possession, his arms enfolding her as passion subsided and she floated tranquilly back down to earth.

She couldn't remember ever having felt so relaxed, so good about herself, her body bathed in a tired but completely pleasurable sense of satisfaction. She turned her head to look at Race and froze as she saw the expression of bitter disbelief in his eyes.

'That was your first time, wasn't it?'

Whatever she had expected from him it wasn't this. What she had expected—and yes, she might as well admit it—was for him to exhibit a certain sense of pleasure in being her first, indeed her only lover. But instead he seemed bitterly angry, as angry as though she had knowingly deprived him of something.

'Does it matter?' She tried to say the words lightly, but instead they merely sounded huskily pleading.

'Does it matter?' She felt him withdraw from her. 'Of course it damned well does,' he said roughly. 'Why didn't you tell me?'

'When?' Heather asked acidly, her euphoria quickly dissipating in the coldness of his manner towards her. She badly wanted to cry, but she wasn't going to. How could he be so hard as to question her like this, after what they had just shared? Only, of course, it wasn't anything special to him. No more and possibly much less than he had enjoyed with countless other women.

'It's hardly the sort of gambit with which one can open a conversation, is it?' she said bitterly. '*Oh, by the way, I'm a virgin?*'

'There were other occasions.'

'Like when you were accusing me of being a tease? Or when you were talking about all my other men? When?'

'When you realised I was treating you as a woman with considerable sexual experience,' Race said brutally, watching her flinch. 'God, you surely don't think I would have. . . .'

'Made love to me?' Heather implemented, her chin up as she surveyed him militantly. Wasn't he going to leave her with anything? 'I thought that was the whole object of the exercise!'

'It was,' he assured her grimly, 'but there are ways . . . and that wasn't the way I would have chosen to . . . to initiate a virgin.' He swung round so that he had his back to her, and she wondered what he was really thinking. Had he found her so disappointing? She ought to be feeling shame and despair right now, but all she could feel was anger, anger against Race because he was rejecting the most precious gift she had had to give him.

'Why have you never made love with anyone before?' How dared he ask her that question? was Heather's initial response, followed by the knowledge that she was in very deep water.

'Perhaps no one's asked me,' she began flippantly, her voice fading as she saw the determined look in his eyes. She swallowed and held hard to her courage. 'Perhaps simply because no one's ever aroused me in the way that you do. In fact, I've always taken care that they never got the chance.'

'And now you're blaming propinquity. Well, perhaps you're right,' he muttered, 'and what's done is done, but it's just as well that we should be able to leave here soon.'

At least he hadn't guessed her secret, Heather thought tiredly. This wasn't how she had visualised the evening ending at all. If she was honest she would have to admit that she had envisaged spending it wrapped in Race's arms, sleeping against the warmth of his body, wakening with him in the morning and experiencing again the pleasure of his lovemaking.

Her last thought, as she eventually hovered between sleeping and waking, wrapped up in front of the fire in her solitary sleeping-bag, was that she had never had her champagne after all. But then she scarcely had anything to celebrate. Race had made it brutally clear that he no longer wanted her. Obviously virgins were not a breed he found at all desirable, and she only hoped the thaw would come soon enough for her to leave the cottage with her pride still intact and her love still her own personal secret.

Only now could she admit to herself that she had gambled on securing more than Race's desire, that she had hoped their lovemaking might set alight a love within him that could match her own. Well, she should have known better. She had gambled and lost, and perhaps it would teach her what was obviously a well needed lesson. Hadn't she learned years ago that no man could love her? She would have been wise to bear that lesson in mind tonight.

CHAPTER SEVEN

'HEATHER, I didn't expect to see you back so soon.'

'I'm sure you didn't,' Heather agreed dryly, as her cousin opened the flat door a little wider. 'But as I am here, how about letting me in?'

'Of course. Oh, you poor thing!' Jennifer exclaimed. 'You look exhausted! When did you leave Scotland? Did. . . .'

'This morning, and yes, I did see Race,' Heather agreed dryly, her composure abandoning her for a moment as she exclaimed huskily, 'Oh, Jen, how could you?'

'I know, I'm sorry,' Jennifer apologised as she helped her in, taking her case. 'Mum's already torn a strip off me. Oh, I told her all about it after you'd gone. How I was sure you were in love with Race and that he wasn't exactly indifferent to you. Mum said you'd be furious with me, and rightly, but he was so persuasive.' This last comment ended on a wail, and Heather had to fight down the memory of exactly how persuasive Race Williams could be when it suited him.

'What happened between you?' Jennifer begged. 'You were supposed to stay up there for two months. When you didn't come straight back I thought I must have done the right thing and that all you needed was some time alone together to sort out your differences.'

'We were snowed in together, otherwise I'd have come straight back,' Heather told her coolly, anxious for there to be no more mistakes or misunderstandings. When Race eventually returned to London, she didn't

want to be embarrassed by Jennifer constantly trying
to throw the two of them together. . . .

'So it didn't work, then?'

'There was nothing to work,' Heather stressed. 'Jen,
Race wanted me sexually, but he doesn't love me,
and. . . .'

'And you love him,' Jen supplied softly. 'Oh God,
Heather, I'm so sorry. Has he come back with you?'

Heather shook her head. 'No. He had work to do,
and I decided, that is. . . .' She bit her lip guiltily, not
wanting to think about that final morning they had
shared. The situation had grown intolerable after Race
had rejected her and she had welcomed the thaw
which had come two days later. Race had gone to the
MacNeils to borrow their Range-Rover and had driven
her into the village to her car. They had parted
without words, without any acknowledgement of what
had happened between them, Heather too proud to
refer to it and Race still too angry. She hadn't allowed
herself the luxury of tears on the journey back, and
now her eyes felt gritty with them, her throat aching.

'Oh, Heather, I can't tell you how sorry I am,'
Jennifer said remorsefully, and Heather knew her cousin
wasn't merely referring to having tricked her. 'I haven't
dared ring Mum since,' she admitted, 'you know what
she's like when she gets mad. She's ten times more
protective of you than she is of me. Do you know what
she said to me? She said you were too vulnerable and
that sometimes she was frightened for you.'

The salt taste of tears stung the back of Heather's
throat. Her aunt knew her better than she had
thought; had she known all these years how much of
an outsider she had still felt, how much in some
strange way she had felt excluded by her parents'
death, as though they had gone somewhere together
where she could not follow and wasn't welcome?

Banishing the thought, Heather went into the kitchen and filled the kettle. She had felt quite nauseous on the drive home, probably because she hadn't stopped for anything to eat, but she simply couldn't have faced it. It had been strange, driving south and seeing the snow give way to winter green fields and bare trees. What was Race doing now? Driving into Fort William to find a woman more experienced than she was herself? He had laughed bitterly when she had told him she was leaving, telling her brutally that he was glad. She ought to hate him, but she didn't, she couldn't even raise the energy to hate herself. All she felt was a vast, unending emptiness.

She phoned her agent when she had been home for two days to tell him of her decision to give up modelling entirely. He had been stunned and then disbelieving, until she had made it clear that she wasn't going to change her mind.

'But what *are* you going to do?' Jennifer asked her one evening as they sat eating their supper and watching television. Jennifer had been out with Terry, and her face had the soft, vulnerable look of a woman in love.

'Who knows? Fate will show me the way,' Heather said humorously, never dreaming how prophetic her words were to prove. Since her return to London she had felt listless and spent, unable to do anything more than simply exist.

When the phone rang one afternoon and she answered it to hear her aunt, she wondered wryly if Jennifer's machinations had been behind the phone call. She knew how guilty Jennifer felt about her part in throwing her into Race's company, and sensed that her cousin was trying her best to make amends.

'Heather darling, I was wondering if you could

spare me a few days,' her aunt asked her. 'Your uncle hasn't been well. It's this nasty 'flu epidemic that's been going round, and Dr Barnes says he's got to spend at least a week in bed. Neil's doing his best at the office, of course, but the work is piling up and I've promised I'll help out if I can. The only problem is, who is going to look after your uncle?'

Heather's uncle owned the local estate agents firm, and Neil was his junior partner. Before the children had come along, her aunt had worked in the business and still occasionally lent a hand when things got busy. 'With spring just round the corner it's one of our busiest times,' she heard her aunt saying worriedly. 'I just don't know what we're going to do if you can't come.'

In all the years she had lived with them this was the first time Heather had heard anything approaching panic in her placid aunt's voice, and she wondered wryly if she really was needed. She promised to think about it and let her aunt have her answer the following day. Before she committed herself she would phone Neil and find out just what was going on. She rang the office several times, but on each occasion only got the answering service which seemed to confirm her aunt's comments. When Jennifer came home, she looked so genuinely surprised and worried that Heather felt guilty for even thinking of doubting her family.

'Look, Terry and I are going out to a charity do tonight. Why don't you come with us? You haven't been out once since you got back,' Jennifer scolded her. 'And if you're going to bury yourself in the country you ought to have at least one brief fling before you go. Believe me, Heather,' she added seriously, 'I have been there—I understand how much you want to be on your own, but it won't do any good. In fact . . .' she bit her lip and then admitted wryly,

'I've already been asked by at least half a dozen people at work if it's true that you and Race have a thing going. Once it gets out that you're back in London, hiding yourself away, you can imagine the conclusions that will be drawn, and Race is bound. . . .'

'To guess how I feel about him?' Heather interposed bitterly. 'Yes, you're right, Jen. Does anyone know about . . . that we. . . .'

'No,' Jennifer assured her. 'Word has it that Race is abroad somewhere working on his latest book—he owns a villa in the Cayman Islands, apparently. There have been murmurs that you might be out there with him. The way he looked at you at the do we had wasn't exactly something you could miss, but I've dropped hints that you've been on a modelling trip.'

Jennifer was right. If people were already gossiping about her and Race, if she continued to hide herself away they could guess that he had ditched her, and her pride couldn't endure the speculation that would follow.

The charity ball was being held at the Dorchester, and Heather dressed accordingly in an Anthony Price gown—there was really no other way to describe it—that she had modelled for him for an advertising feature, and which he had later sold to her at cost price. Even then it had been horrendously expensive, and as she was zipping it up she had a moment's bitter memory of Race calling her 'gypsy girl', which she banished firmly as she studied her reflection and tried not to think of how much she deserved the title in this dress of rich gold satin with its low-cut bodice that moulded her breasts, the off-the-shoulder sleeves trimmed lavishly with écru lace bows which matched the trim round the hem.

She had swept her hair to one side and secured it with a gold comb, using her model-girl skill to emphasise her high cheekbones and the depth and size of her eyes. When she had finished she looked every inch the wild gypsy girl, and Jennifer's eyes widened in admiration as she walked in to see if she was ready.

'Wow,' she exclaimed, 'talk about the lord and the lady! All we need is for some dashing young Lochinvar to sweep you off on his steed . . . .'

'Not at the Dorchester,' Heather told her dryly. 'What time is the taxi due to arrive?'

It arrived five minutes later, having already collected Terry who greeted them both with a warm smile, but the kiss he bestowed on Jennifer was anything but friendly, Heather thought, watching them with a mixture of envy and amusement.

The ballroom was packed with famous faces; Heather recognised a score of fellow models and half the media world in its differing guises, plus an assortment of peers and politicians as well as famous names from the world of commerce.

She danced in turn with a baronet, a pop singer and a captain of industry, any one of whom would have been delighted to do more than simply dance, but Heather kept them all at bay with her normal cool smile until the moment she turned and saw Race watching her not three yards away, his eyes mocking her as they slid indolently over her body. In a dream she saw him walk towards her, conscious of Jennifer hurrying to her side, Terry in tow, and her escort looking none too pleased at Race's approach. A newspaper gossip columnist she had recognised was watching them, and Heather felt her heart thud in mingled pain and pleasure as she studied Race; evening clothes suited him, but then what didn't? Tonight he looked sleek and debonair, totally at home in his surroundings, the blonde girl he was partnering clinging possessively to his arm as they approached.

'Hello, gypsy lady.' No one apart from themselves could know the meaning of his words, no one apart from herself could know the pain they caused her. She forced herself to smile, conscious of exploding flashlights and interested glances. Jenny was right, she and Race were in danger of becoming a gossip item.

'Hello, Race.' Somehow she managed to stay cool, extending her hand in a perfunctory greeting, introducing him to her escort, acknowledging his introduction to the simpering blonde she suddenly hated with white-hot searing jealousy, especially when the sickly-sweet voice cooed softly, 'Darling, you promised me we wouldn't need to stay long. I want to go home . . . with you, darling.'

Red lips pouted and Heather felt a wave of nausea attack her as she looked down into the other girl's face. Five foot two and as fragile as Dresden—of course!

'I'll bet she isn't a virgin.' Heather wasn't aware that she had muttered the words, until she saw Race's eyebrows rise.

'No,' he agreed equably, adding with devastating cruelty, 'thank God.'

Telling herself that she was lucky that no one else had been close enough to overhear the small exchange, Heather let her partner lead her back to the dance floor. All she wanted to do was to run, to be somewhere alone, but pride kept her where she was, talking, dancing, drinking and pretending to eat until she could reasonably go home.

She was in bed when Jennifer returned, and Heather suppressed a small stab of envy when she saw her cousin's flushed, happy face.

'Terry's proposed,' she announced happily. 'Oh, Heather, I never thought he would! I'm so happy I'm going to cry,' she moaned, promptly doing exactly that.'

'That's not happiness, it's champagne,' Heather told her pithily, softening her words with a swift hug. Her own mind was made up. Now that she knew Race was back in London she must leave. Her aunt's plea for help gave her the ideal, genuine excuse.

She told Jennifer over breakfast—a breakfast she felt totally unable to eat. She had felt most unwell when she woke up and had put it down to a surfeit of nervous dread and too much alcohol the previous night. Now she felt almost light-headed.

She left London at lunchtime, having decided that once her uncle was well she was going to ask him to find her a small house. She had enough money not to need to work, but she had her book to occupy her mind and she had always been interested in antiques, perhaps she might even buy herself a small business.

Neil was at the station to meet her, enveloping her in a hard hug. Although smaller than she was in their early teens, the twins had both overtaken her. Neil was six foot two, and he laughed as he swung her off the ground, pulling her hair which she had confined in a long plait.

'You've lost weight,' he told her accusingly as he opened the car door. 'Something wrong?'

She and Neil had always been particularly close. It was he who had started her off on her modelling career and who had encouraged her with her writing. Despite his outer ruggedness, Neil was extremely sensitive to other people's emotional needs, and Heather longed to pour her misery out to him, to tell him how she felt, but pride restrained her. She had left all that behind in London, and had no intention of resurrecting it either.

'I'm just worried about Uncle Roy,' she fibbed, her comment not entirely untrue. She was worried about her uncle.

'Umm, this bug's hit him hard,' Neil admitted,

suddenly grave. 'It's time he was thinking of retiring, but you know what he's like. Anyway, Dr Barnes has told him there's no question of him coming back to work yet. I think we ought to take on another partner, but I'll have to talk him round to it. We're run off our feet at the moment.'

'Well, anything I can do to help,' Heather assured him. 'Aunt Lydia is going to help out in the office, isn't she?'

'Yep, Ma's a wonder. She knows all the ropes, and it's great having someone reliable to take people on viewing expeditions. Meredew's, the electronics people, have opened a new factory in Tytherton, and we've been inundated with enquiries from their people for property. In fact we're having what you might call a mini-boom.'

Neil enjoyed his work, and Heather forgot her troubles long enough to laugh at his feeling description of a couple who had assured him that their house was worth twice as much as the value he had placed upon it.

'Here we are.'

Her aunt and uncle lived in the edge of a small Cotswold village in a red-brick Queen Anne house which had once been the Vicarage. Heather loved the house and could still vividly remember the first time she had seen it after her parents' death. She had arrived on a wet, cold day, and the house had warmed her with its rosy glow, holding out welcoming arms to enfold her, just as her aunt had done.

Once again she found the same welcome, hugging her small aunt back enthusiastically. 'Jenny told me what she did, and I gave her a real telling off for it,' Lydia told her frankly, when Neil had gone to garage the car. 'She isn't like you, Heather, she doesn't think before she acts. How are you? All right?'

'Shaken and bruised,' Heather admitted, not able to lie to her aunt. 'I fell for him, and hard. He wanted me. . . . I tried to tell myself it wasn't enough. . . .'

There was a degree of frankness between them that Heather cherished. She had always been able to talk to her aunt, but it was not her way to make use of anyone else as a confidante, and she came to an abrupt halt, colouring as she realised how much she was giving away.

'It's all right, Heather, I do understand. . . .' her aunt assured her. 'I appreciate that it sounds trite, but I was young once myself, and very, very deeply in love—madly in love, was I suppose the right term. It was before I met your uncle. He, John, was an airman at one of the local bases. It was towards the end of the war, and a hectic sense of urgency it isn't easy to describe nowadays possessed us all. I loved him and I wanted him,' she told Heather simply, 'and I've never been sorry or guilty about what we shared, although I suppose it could have been different if. . . .' She broke off to chastise her son as he came into the immaculate kitchen without wiping his feet, accepting Heather's offer of taking her uncle a cup of tea, gratefully, as the telephone started to ring.

Any doubts she might have had about being needed at home were banished when Heather saw how fragile her uncle looked. He greeted her with a beam, patting the chair at the side of his bed. 'At last, someone who'll have a few minutes to talk to me. How are you, lass?'

'Fine,' Heather assured him huskily. 'Unlike you. You've been working too hard.'

'Who told you that? Dr Barnes?' He's an old woman, always has been. I'd feel a lot better if I could get up and see what young Neil's doing,' he grumbled, as Heather plumped his pillows and sat with him while he drank his tea.

Later when they were alone she admitted to Neil how shocked she had been to see how frail his father was.

'Oh, he's tougher than he looks,' Neil assured her. 'He's over the worst of it now. You worry too much,' he told her gently, 'you always did. I can still remember the way you broke your heart over that blackbird the cat got.'

Heather could remember the incident vividly. The family's cat had brought home a young blackbird with a broken wing. At her insistence Neil had rescued it and they had kept the bird in a shoe box in the greenhouse. Every day Heather had urged it to get better, but every day it had grown a little more weak, until one morning she had found it stiff and cold. Neil had found her, crying as though her heart would break, and she hadn't been able to explain to him that her grief wasn't entirely for the bird. His death had come too soon after the loss of her parents for her to bear it with equanimity, and it had seemed to her that no sooner did she love something than it was taken away from her. She had grown obsessive about her new-found family, fearing almost with every breath she took that something might happen to them, but of course it hadn't, and gradually she had learned to accept.

'You were always such a passionate little thing,' Neil teased, startling her with his observation. She had always thought of herself as cool and controlled. 'Perhaps not outwardly,' he added, watching her, 'but inside, in there.' He tapped her chest lightly, and then abandoning all pretence said quietly, 'Heather, what's wrong?—and don't fob me off, I know it isn't just Pa. Something's wrong. What is it? A man?'

She couldn't tell him. She shook her head, half blinded with tears, glad of her aunt's appearance to bring an end to their conversation.

Within a week of her arrival her uncle was well on the road to recovery, but Heather felt consistently ill. She was tired all the time and suffered from recurring bouts of nausea, her mind and body so lethargic that everything was an effort.

One morning when she had overslept, she hurried downstairs, to be caught up in a bout of sickness so compelling that it stopped her in the hall, her face pale and damp with perspiration, as she fought down the horrible sensation.

The kitchen door opened just as she was overwhelmed by a feeling of dizziness, and she was dimly aware of Neil's arms going round her, his deep voice anxious as he called his mother. Half an hour later Heather was ensconced in a comfortable chair sipping weak tea, and eating the biscuit her aunt had insisted would make her feel better, Neil hovering anxiously at her side.

'I don't know what's the matter with me,' she admitted to her aunt. 'I haven't felt well for days.' She saw the look mother and son exchanged and felt herself tense. It was almost as though an unspoken message passed between them.

'Neil, go and fill my cup up for me, will you?' his mother asked calmly. When he had gone she turned to Heather and said softly, 'Oh, Heather, my dear, for a very intelligent girl I'm beginning to think you're behaving rather like an ostrich. I suspect you're pregnant,' she said calmly. 'Could that be true?'

Pregnant! Heather reeled. But of course! Of course she was. She counted back slowly, wondering how on earth she could have been so blind, so stupid. She had been so caught up in what she felt about Race that she had never even contemplated anything like this. Presumably, thinking her experienced, he had looked to her to take whatever precautions she deemed necessary. Race's child! A queer little thrill of pleasure darted through her.

'I think it might be,' she told her aunt shakily, suddenly giving way to tears and burying her head in her hands. 'Oh, Aunt Lydia, I never thought. . . .'

'One seldom does,' her aunt agreed dryly. 'I'm not going to ask you what you're going to do. Think carefully about it, Heather. I know I'm from a different generation and you must, of course, do what you think fit, but, except in exceptional cases, my feeling is that life is a precious and very rare gift. You're not a schoolgirl, or even a foolish teenager, and if you should decide that you can't cope with the responsibility of a child, then you know that your uncle and I will do all that we can to help you. If, on the other hand you decide to keep the baby . . . well, you can still be sure of our love and support. I take it there's no chance of a marriage. . . .'

'No, not the slightest,' Heather assured her bleakly. 'I won't even tell him about the baby. It . . . it wouldn't be fair. It wasn't what he intended, and the fault,' she grimaced, 'is all mine.'

Unacknowledged but there between them was the hesitant admission that she would let her pregnancy take its course, and as the day wore on and she had more time to think about and come to terms with it, Heather's resolve strengthened. She might have an abortion, but did she have the strength of mind to cope with the guilt she would suffer afterwards? There was no easy answer, either way there would be pain, but at least there would also be pleasure in bearing Race's child. Did she have the right to bring it into the world, though, without the care and love of its father?

Thousands of other girls coped in similar circumstances, somehow she would find the strength to do
the same. She had money, the support of her family.

The subject wasn't mentioned again. Heather paid a
discreet visit to Dr Barnes' surgery, and waited
nervously for the results of her tests, surprised to
discover how pleased she was to discover they were
positive and that she was carrying Race's child. A
warm smile curved her mouth as her fingertips
touched lightly against her still flat stomach. Race's
child, some small part of him which would always be
hers.

Her uncle was now up and about although still off
work, and Heather decided that she would tell her
family her decision over dinner.

She waited until her aunt had poured the coffee, and
then told them simply and calmly.

'I'm very glad, dear,' her aunt responded kissing her
cheek. 'I'm not going to deny that I wish it hadn't
happened—not for our sake, but for yours, but
knowing you as I do, I don't think you could have
coped mentally with the emotional aspects of an
abortion.'

Her uncle looked slightly discomfited and Neil, who
had said nothing to her about it since the morning he
found her being sick in the hall, got up and hugged
her tightly. 'We'll do all we can to help,' he promised
her. 'Bags I be godfather! Just wait until I tell Rich!'

His twin was away in Australia working for a
mineral exploration company, and Heather felt her
mood lighten, tears stinging her eyes as she thought of
how lucky she was in her family.

'Uncle Roy, I want to buy a small house—I think
it's better if I move away—not too far away,' she
promised her aunt, 'but it's bound to be embarrassing
for you.'

She bit her lip, unable to continue, laughing shakily when her aunt said robustly, 'Nothing of the sort. My dear Heather, it's positively trendy these days to have a daughter, sans husband but very much with child, about the place.'

'What will you do about Jen?' Neil asked. 'You know what a blabbermouth she can be,' he added with brotherly candour. 'I take it she does know who the father is?'

They were on their own in the garden, Heather having gone there for a breath of fresh air, and he had followed her.

'What makes you think *I* know?' she asked dryly, and was rewarded by a flash of anger in the dark blue eyes.

'It's Neil, Heather, remember?' he said brusquely. 'I know you, and I know damned well that until you met this man you were still a virgin. Oh, come on,' he said softly when she blushed. 'I grew up with you—remember? You were always a princess dreaming in an ivory tower, inviolate and pure. Whoever he is, he must be quite someone.'

'He is,' Heather agreed on a sigh, 'but someone who doesn't feel about me the way I feel about him.'

In the end her dilemma with regard to Jennifer was solved when the latter appeared at the weekend with Terry in tow. They had come down to announce their engagement, and Jennifer took Heather on one side to tell her that she had done the right thing in leaving London.

'He's currently escorting Lady Davinia Fane and they're making all the gossip columns, but I'm betting it won't last. I'm sorry, Heather,' she apologised, 'but I thought he genuinely cared about you. You did the right thing to leave. If you'd stayed looking the way you do at the moment you might just as well tell the whole world how you feel about him. By the way,' she added curiously, 'what's got into big brother Neil? He always did have a watch-dog approach towards you, but now. . . .' she pulled a wry face and said, 'he's already been cross-questioning me about you, who your friends are, etc., etc.'

Heather realised she would have to tell her cousin the truth. 'I'm pregnant, Jen,' she announced baldly. 'Everyone else knows, but I haven't told them the name of the father.'

'Pregnant?' Jennifer's eyes were like saucers. 'What are you going to do? Get rid of it?' Heather winced and saw Jennifer pull a wry face. 'Yes, I know, hardly delicate, am I? and knowing you, I was crass too—of course you won't. I take it you don't intend Race to know?'

'What would be the point?' Heather asked tiredly. 'He didn't want me before, and he's even less likely to want me now. No, this baby is mine, Jen, my responsibility, mine completely. . . .'

'Except for the fact that Race fathered it,' Jennifer pointed out mildly, 'and I wouldn't be so sure if I were you. You say he won't want the baby—I'm not so sure. I think you could find he has very strong views about his child.'

'If he does I'm hardly likely to find out. Please don't meddle this time, Jen,' she warned. 'I don't want him to know. Give me your word you won't say anything.'

Not until Jennifer gave it was she satisfied. The knowledge that Jennifer could be right when she said Race might have strong views about any child he fathered made her feel uneasy. This child was hers, the only thing she had left, and she intended to keep it.

CHAPTER EIGHT

BOTH her aunt and uncle firmly refused to allow her to look for anywhere else to live, and their warmth and love were so comforting that Heather soon ceased to fight against them. Contrary to her expectations there were no whispered comments when she walked through the village, even when the flatness of her stomach began to blur, and her shape in the thin cotton dresses she had taken to wearing as spring drifted towards summer was quite distinctly that of a pregnant woman. She felt oddly contented; time seemed to merge and although she was aware of pain, of loneliness and heartache because there was no Race, nature, ever protective of her handiwork, gave her a layer of insulation against the pain. The baby started to kick and she smiled tremulously to feel the small arms and legs moving angrily, convinced that the child must be a boy. Neil teased and petted her, refusing to let her hide herself away, insisting that she accompany him to their local pub, taking her out to dinner, until she was forced to tell him gently that people would begin to think the child was his.

'No way,' he assured her softly, placing his palm against her rounded stomach, its warmth making the baby kick hard. 'If this was mine you'd be wearing my ring, Heather—and sometimes I wish to God you were,' he told her forcefully. 'I know it's useless, and I've had a long time to learn acceptance. I think I first fell in love with you when I saw you sitting up in the apple tree, covered in scratches because you'd gone after a kitten. I wanted to take you in my arms then and make you better.'

'Instead of which you bawled me out until I cried,' Heather remembered. 'Oh, Neil, I never knew. . . .'

'I never intended you to,' he said steadily. 'I'm a realist, Heather, and I accept that I love you because I haven't yet met the girl who can displace you. One day I hope I will. Until then, believe me, I have no objection to the whole world thinking that's my child inside you.'

He raised her fingers to his lips, kissing them lightly, leaving her with an aching sense of waste and futility. Neil loved her, and she had never known, might never have known. And it was all such a waste, because she could never love him back, not in the same way.

As the year blossomed so did her body. May was warm with soft blue skies and light breezes, and her aunt commented that never had the adjective 'blooming' had such an apt application. 'Don't become too wrapped up in this baby, though, Heather,' she warned her niece as they sat in the shade of the chestnut tree in the garden, the lawn scattered with remnants of the pink blossom. 'Leave room in your life for other people.'

Heather knew her aunt meant another man, but she didn't say anything. There would be no other man, at least not one who could come anywhere near taking Race's place in her heart, she was reasonably certain of that.

Neil arrived just as they were finishing their tea. He flopped down on the lawn at Heather's feet, leaning back, supporting his head with his interlocked hands. 'I think I've sold the Radford place,' he told them. 'It's been on the market for just over eighteen months, but it looks very much as though we've found a buyer.'

'Your father will be pleased,' his mother agreed.

'Umm, *I* certainly am. It was beginning to become something of an albatross. Fancy celebrating with me?' he asked Heather.

'In this condition?' she laughed down at him.

'Why not? You aren't in purdah, merely pregnant. I know you're not ashamed about the baby, so that must mean you're ashamed of being seen with me. What's the matter? Aren't I good enough to be considered its father?'

He got up and strode angrily into the house, and although the sun still shone Heather felt as though a shadow had fallen across the afternoon. She looked at her aunt. She was very still, unhappiness in her eyes.

'He's wrong,' Heather told her huskily, 'it's not that, it's just. . . .'

'That you don't love him the way he loves you. I know, my dear, and I'm glad you have the honesty to tell him. Oh yes, I know how he feels about you.' Lydia smiled wryly. 'Mothers generally do.'

'It would be much better if I found somewhere else to live,' Heather said unhappily, 'If I wasn't constantly under his feet. . . .'

She noticed that although her aunt shook her head, she didn't argue with her. It was bad for Neil having her living in the same house with him, and she suffered with him, knowing all too well the pain of unrequited love. But Neil was a man and essentially more practical than any woman could ever be. If he could find someone else he would forget her. . . . But he wouldn't allow himself to find someone else. His attitude towards the coming baby was getting distinctly proprietorial, and Heather knew she was going to have to look for somewhere else to live. Affording her own home was no problem, but she liked living with her aunt and uncle; she enjoyed their company, and Neil's.

She was being selfish, she told herself later that night as she prepared for bed. Dr Barnes had told her that she was underweight the last time she went for a check-up, although he had been quick to assure her that the baby was fine. 'Better too little than too much,' they had said at the hospital, meanwhile encouraging her to eat a little more.

'I'm going into Gloucester today, why not come with me?' Neil suggested over breakfast. There was no trace of his bad mood of the day before and Heather hesitated before accepting, before thinking that it would be a good opportunity for her to visit several estate agents in the town and to tell Neil of her decision to find a house of her own.

They set out immediately after breakfast, Neil taking care to make sure she was safely installed in his car. He was treating her like rare, fragile glass, and her heart ached because it wasn't Race who was at her side, tenderly careful of her because she carried his child. Race! A day didn't go by without her thinking of him; without her wondering what he was doing, but she had resolutely refused to question Jen, telling herself that this way it was easier and that hearing about him, talking about him could only add to her torment.

They found a parking spot without too much difficulty, and Heather was amused when Neil insisted that they went and had a cup of coffee before they started on their chores. She had several items to collect for her aunt, and Neil had some photographic equipment he wanted to collect from the specialist shop he used. Photography was still his main hobby, and she couldn't help noticing the happiness in the smile the girl behind the counter gave him as they walked in, although it faded a little when she saw Heather.

'Heather, meet Sue,' Neil introduced when he had finished saying 'hello'. 'Her father owns this shop.'

'I'm Neil's cousin,' Heather told her, taking pity on her and feeling her heart contract. Why, oh, why wasn't life more simple? Why can't we love those who love us?

'Nice girl,' Heather commented when they left the shop, adding slyly, 'You used to be rather partial to blondes.'

'I've booked us a table at the Grand for lunch,' Neil told her, ignoring her teasing comment, 'but first we have a very special errand to run. Come with me.'

Heather had no suspicion of what he intended until they came to the small and very expensive baby specialist shop tucked down a narrow street. Pastel-coloured continental clothes and equipment adorned the window, but Heather hesitated and would have pulled back if Neil hadn't taken her arm and pushed her gently inside.

'Neil. . . .' she began to protest, but he simply shook his head and whispered, 'He's going to be my godson, Heather, remember? Besides,' he added impishly, 'you know I've always preferred sporty models, and when I take him for a walk, I don't particularly fancy pushing the Vicar's niece's old jalopy.'

Mary Simmonds, the Vicar's niece, had offered Heather the pram her two children had outgrown, and Heather had accepted it, telling herself it would be an extravagance to buy a new one. But now, in this shop filled with the most expensive and elegant equipment money could buy, she felt like a very small child let loose in a sweet shop. It was ridiculous to get so excited at the thought of a mere pram, and she turned quickly to tell Neil that she wasn't going to allow him to buy her one, when her attention was caught by a man walking purposefully down the street. He was wearing dark-coloured pants and a thin cotton shirt which moulded itself to his body as the breeze caught it. A faint feeling of disbelief swept over Heather as she watched him. It was Race, she knew it was!

A deep trembling began inside her, her entire attention concentrated on the tall, dark-haired man walking along the street. He paused and she got her first glimpse of his features. It *was* Race. What was he doing in Gloucester? She half expected him to look into the shop and see her, and time seemed to stand still for an eternity while she waited for him to do so, but he didn't. And she saw him gradually disappear from view, her heart labouring in pain and disappointment.

'Heather, what's wrong?' Neil's voice was sharply concerned, his eyes shadowed with worry. 'The baby?'

'No . . . no, it's nothing. I just felt a little bit faint,' she fibbed. Race here; Race so close that she could almost have touched him. Pain curled and exploded inside her, tearing her apart making her long to run after him. She was behaving like a hysterical teenager, she upbraided herself, trying to concentrate on what Neil was saying, but she couldn't force herself to pay attention, and it was only as they left the shop that she realised that she had let Neil talk her into having the most expensive pram they had.

He watched her closely over lunch, and his concern was like a warm, comforting quilt, insulating her from the rest of the world, but what was the use of a quilt when all she longed for was the abrasive reality of Race?

On their way back to the car they had to pass the offices of the local paper, and knowing that Neil sometimes contributed photographs to it, Heather paused, her face paling as she recognised her own face staring back at her from several they had on display.

But the Heather Neil had portrayed was a far cry from the model girl she had been. He had photographed her lying under the chestnut tree, the light cotton of her dress doing nothing to conceal her pregnancy, but it was her face that caught her eye, the vulnerable, dreaming expression in her eyes, and the soft pleasure of her mouth. One hand rested possessively on her stomach and it seemed to Heather that ·the photograph shrieked of her satisfaction in carrying Race's child, her eyes warm with remembered pleasure at the begetting of it.

'Oh, Neil, how could you?' she expostulated, feeling her face colour. The photograph had been taken in a private and unguarded moment, and just looking at it made Heather feel acutely vulnerable.

'I couldn't resist,' Neil said huskily. 'To me you epitomise everything that's womanly in a woman, Heather.' And to her consternation he bent his head and kissed her lightly on the lips before letting her go, and for all the fact that she was nearly as tall as he was himself Heather had never felt quite as feminine and protected in all her life.

And therein lay the danger, she thought wryly as they walked back to the car. Neil was giving her all the care and attention she would have loved to get from Race, and wasn't she in danger of relying on him too much, of using him to bolster her courage, which wasn't fair on him?

'Even like this, men still fancy you,' Neil told her with a grin as they reached the end of the street. 'When I kissed you just then, there was a guy watching us as though he'd like to slit my throat!'

'Perhaps he didn't know we were just kissing cousins,' Heather said lightly, disengaging her fingers from him.

'Is that all we are, Heather?'

She took a deep breath and turned to face him. 'You know it is, Neil,' she answered firmly. 'I love you—as a brother.'

'And I love you as a woman.' He sounded bitter, angry almost, and Heather felt a momentary pang. How simple it would be to give in, to let Neil take over and shield her all her life with his love! But then she remembered seeing Race. That one brief glance had been enough to reactivate all she had felt for him, and she knew that her affection for Neil was only a pale shadow of her love for Race. She couldn't cheat them both by pretending otherwise.

Race. What had he been doing in Gloucester? She toyed with the idea of ringing Jen, and then dismissed it, telling herself that she was only torturing herself by doing that.

Neil insisted on them making a detour on the way back, and they stopped at one of the Cotswold villages for Heather to stretch her legs.

Her aunt seemed unusually flustered when they got back. She had had a phone call from some old friends who apparently wanted them to drive over and have lunch with them the following day.

'Pa won't like that,' Neil told her laconically, helping himself to a handful of the salad she was preparing. 'He always plays golf on Sunday mornings.'

'Well, tomorrow you're going to have to stand in for me,' his father announced, walking in almost on cue. 'It's all arranged,' he added when Neil started to protest, 'your mother is insisting that I go with her, and I can't let Reg Barnes down now. Besides, you enjoy a game.'

'I had planned to take Heather out for a run tomorrow,' Neil protested, and Heather, not wanting to spoil her aunt and uncle's plans, said quickly, 'Oh no, Neil, I had planned to look at some houses tomorrow.'

She saw his face and added quietly, 'I think it's for the best, and. . . .'

'No, Heather, you mustn't do any such thing on your own,' she heard her aunt insist firmly, much to her surprise. 'Now you must promise me you will stay here tomorrow, I wouldn't have a moment's peace if I thought you were tramping up and down flights of stairs on your own.'

In the end Heather gave way. She could tell that Neil wasn't at all pleased at her decision, but what else could she do? If only he could meet someone else— but he was hardly likely to do that, she admitted wryly, when he insisted on sticking to her side like glue.

She was up early in the morning, unable to sleep, tormented by images of Race, all her love and longing for him resurrected by that one brief sight of him. What had he been doing? She nibbled her bottom lip as she made the breakfast, wondering if she was right in thinking that the Fane family had a property in the Cotswolds. Could that be it? Could he be staying with Lady Davinia, and her family? She tried not to admit the anguish the thought brought, wandering restlessly round the large family kitchen as she waited for her aunt and uncle to come down.

Her aunt seemed tense and almost nervous over breakfast. She kept darting glances at Heather, and Heather suspected she was probably worrying that she might break her promise. 'Look, I won't put a foot outside the garden,' she assured her affectionately. 'Stop worrying.'

They were doing the washing-up together when her aunt said suddenly, 'Heather, you know that I love you as though you were my own, don't you? I always wanted another daughter, and you're very precious to me . . . to us both. If I thought . . .' she broke off, and Heather wondered if she was trying to talk to her about Neil. There was no need, she could guess how torn her aunt was, wanting what was best for both of them.

'Everything will work out,' she told her, trying to sound comforting. 'You just wait and see. . . .'

She was rewarded with a rather vague smile, and when she waved her aunt and uncle off an hour later she was left with the distinct impression that something was worrying the former.

Neil had already gone, and knowing Dr Barnes of old and his addiction to the golf course, Heather guessed he wouldn't be back until much later in the afternoon. Not that she minded. It was almost a luxury to have the house and garden to herself. The air was warm with the promise of summer to come, her uncle's well-tended garden a mass of blooms. The new leaves on the chestnut tree were freshly green, and after she had finished tidying her room, Heather gazed out at it, tempted to go and lie in the sun.

Her body had changed during her pregnancy, and she studied it thoughtfully as she slipped off her clothes and took clean panties and dress from her wardrobe. Her breasts felt slightly tender, her nipples darker, her skin silky smooth. The thought of holding Race's child in her arms made her tremble with longing; there was an unmistakably primitive pleasure to be found in the knowledge that her body was flowering with Race's child, she acknowledged wryly, still finding it vaguely surprising that she should be capable of such earthy thoughts and desires. She had always thought of herself as cool, even perhaps genuinely not capable of finding much pleasure in sex, until she met Race. Now barely a night went by without her aching for him; without her longing to wake up and find herself in his arms.

Suppressing a sigh, she dressed slowly, enjoying the feeling of the cool cotton against her skin and the freedom from the restriction of her bra. The cotton did little to conceal the shape of her body, but it scarcely mattered; she had plenty of time to get changed before Neil was due back.

A book she had got for her aunt from the library caught her eye and she took it into the garden with her, using the cushion off one of the garden chairs as a pillow for her head as she stretched out beneath the shelter of the chestnut tree, lulled by the smooth sound of the breeze amongst the leaves. It was blissfully relaxing just lying here, suspended between waking and sleeping, the warm, growing scent of the garden all around her, birdsong a distant and pleasing refrain, the ground warm beneath her fingers, the sun warm on her skin.

She didn't know what woke her. One moment she had been deeply asleep, the next she was wide awake, conscious that something had disturbed her tranquillity.

'Hello, Heather.'

Her eyes shot open, her body tensing in disbelief.

'Race?' He was standing in front of her, long, muscled legs clad in faded denim, a cotton shirt open almost to the waist, his eyes shadowed and remote as he studied her recumbent form.

'What are you doing here?'

'Looking for you.'

'For me? But. . . .' Her thoughts whirled in disjointed disorder. Had Jennifer broken her promise to her? Why had Race come? Had he thought it might be amusing to pay a visit on her while he was in the area? She gasped suddenly as the baby kicked—hard.

'Heather? Heather, are you all right?' He was down

on his knees beside her, his fingers curling against her shoulders in the old, remembered way. She would know Race's touch anywhere, she thought achingly; even without seeeing his face her body would recognise him.

'I'm fine,' she assured him, 'the ... the baby kicked,' she added huskily, unable to look at him. 'What are you doing here, Race?'

'I saw your photograph in the paper. I have some friends who live near Gloucester. I've been spending a few days with them and I saw it.'

'So Jen didn't. . . .' Heather bit her lip, and saw his face harden into anger.

'No, damn her, she didn't,' he said harshly. 'She wouldn't even give me your address, or tell me where you were.'

What had he wanted to know that for? Had he felt guilty about her, perhaps? What did it matter now? The baby kicked again and she placed her hand automatically over the small bump.

'God, Heather, why didn't you tell me?'

She didn't pretend not to know what he meant, or to deny his words, and was glad she hadn't seconds later when he said hoarsely, 'When I saw that damned photograph, saw you like this. . . . I knew the child must be mine. I damn near tore the place apart looking for you. I got your address from the newspaper offices, and I drove down yesterday, but you weren't here. I saw your aunt.'

So that was why her aunt had been so unhappy! She had connived with Race so that he could talk to her alone.

'Why didn't you tell me?' Race repeated slowly. 'Didn't you think I had any right to know?'

'Not really,' she said quietly. 'Let's face it, it was an accident ... my responsibility, because I'm sure you thought that I would have ... taken precautions. There didn't seem any point in telling you,' she added musingly.

'No point? Damn you, Heather!' he suddenly shouted, grasping her shoulders, 'that's my child you're carrying, mine! So don't tell me there wasn't any point. Why did you decide to go on with the pregnancy?' he asked curtly, looking away from her. 'You could have. . . .'

'Had an abortion?' She was angry now. 'Yes I could have, and I suppose from your point of view that would have made life much less ... messy. But you don't need to worry, Race. I absolve you totally from all responsibility. I could have had an abortion, but I didn't choose to. I have enough money to support myself and my child, and. . . .'

'A cousin just ready and waiting to marry you?' he said harshly. 'Oh yes, I know all about that. Well, you might be noble enough to "absolve" me from all responsibility, Heather, but what about my child? Will he or she feel the same way, will they be able to forgive me, or you for that matter, for denying it the right to two parents? Oh, I know it's the fashion for women to take charge of their own lives, do their own thing, bring up their own children on their own. Very nice—for them, but does anyone take into account the views of the kids? Do you know that ninety-five per cent of children of divorced parents, secretly, deep in their hearts, want their parents to get together again?

'I know what it's like not to have a father, Heather. My mother was the forerunner of the modern woman. She chose to have her child alone; her lover was a married man, and she told me once she didn't particularly love him, she just felt the time had come when she had to submit to the biological urge to reproduce. Is that what you're going to tell our child?

Not that it was conceived in love, but out of a "biological urge"? Well, I'm not going to let you. You and I are going to get married, just as soon as it can be arranged. No,' he said sharply when she would have interrupted, 'listen to me. That's my baby growing inside you, and I'll see you in hell before I'll let you deny me my child. We've got some very enlightened judges these days—there are ways I could make you share the child with me, and you know it. Is that what you want? Because I warn you I'm not prepared to simply disappear and let you have it all.'

Marriage to Race! Heather's mind couldn't absorb it. She wanted to refuse; wanted to tell him that she didn't want him without his love. But what about her aunt and uncle? They knew now that Race was the father, wouldn't they want her to marry him? Her aunt would, she knew, although she would never try and influence her decision. And there was Neil to consider. He loved her, but once he saw her as the wife of another man. . . .

And then there were her own feelings. . . . Didn't she secretly long to be Race's wife? Wasn't there a small part of her that clung to the hope that somehow he might come to love her? Perhaps in marriage, sharing their child, love would take root and grow.

'Race, I'll have to have time,' she protested hesitantly. 'I. . . .'

'No.' His voice was thick with suppressed emotion. She had never dreamed he would feel like this. Or had she? Had she always suspected that if he found out about the baby, he would come after her? 'We're both responsible for our child, Heather,' he said unsteadily. 'We've created it, and we owe it our love, *both* of us,' he underlined. 'You must want it or you wouldn't have let your pregnancy continue. Don't you love your child enough to want it to have two parents, to know the security of a proper family unit? You lost both your parents, you must know what that does to a child, just as I know what it's like to grow up without a father. Either you marry me, or I'll take you to court to take the baby away from you, and I'll find someone who *will* marry me!'

'Race. . . .' There was a dark violence in his eyes that shocked her, leaving her feeling helplessly unable to withstand him. 'Race . . . without love . . .' she protested, silenced when he said harshly, 'Oh, but there will be love, won't there, Heather? Love for our child,' and then he bent his head slowly and placed his hand gently on the swollen mound of her stomach, his lips warm against her skin through the thin cotton of her dress.

A strangely unfamiliar emotion rose up inside her, a yearning desire to hold him close and cradle him in her arms as though he were as vulnerable and helpless as their child. She lifted her hand, her fingers stroking softly through the thick darkness of his hair.

'Heather, say yes.' His voice was muffled against her skin, and she knew that she was lost and had been from the moment she opened her eyes and saw him looking down at her.

'Yes,' she said dryly, 'for the. . . .'

'Heather!' She looked up to see Neil striding across the lawn towards them, his face tight with anger and jealousy. 'Heather, what. . . .'

Race got up with one swiftly lithe movement, but Heather couldn't help flushing as she thought how they must have looked to Neil, Race practically cradled in her arms, his head against her breast.

'You must be Neil,' Race said affably before Neil could speak. 'Race Williams . . . your cousin-to-be, and . . .' he glanced down at Heather and smiled mockingly, 'father-to-be, apparently, as well.'

'You . . . bastard!'

The ·bitterness behind the harsh expletive shattered the warm peace of the afternoon and Heather got up clumsily, hating herself for causing Neil pain and intending to go after him and explain, but Race's fingers on her wrist stopped her, his expression tightly angry as he said, 'Let him go, Heather. Sooner or later he's going to have to come to terms with the fact that you and the baby are both mine. . . .'

Which was a rather strange thing to say, Heather thought afterwards, because while Race undoubtedly wanted his child, he surely did not want her. Or had his comment been motivated by pure male sexual jealousy?

Race remained until her aunt and uncle got home, and Heather could tell by the anxious way in which her aunt looked at her that she was worried about Heather's reaction.

'I told your aunt and uncle I intended to marry you,' Race told her as he stood by her side. 'Why did you let them think I wouldn't want my child, Heather?'

'Because I thought that to want a child one must first intend to conceive it,' Heather said dryly. 'Many men in your position wouldn't have wanted it.'

'But you didn't even give me the chance to find out, did you? I suppose that's why Jen was so cagey every time I asked about you, although I admit it took me a few weeks to discover that you'd actually left London and given up modelling.'

And if he had really wanted her he would have come looking for her the moment he came back from Scotland, Heather thought bitterly. But then hadn't she known that all along?

Once Race had got her consent to their wedding he lost no time in making the arrangements. They were to be married by special licence at the local church. Less than a week was hardly adequate time to arrange a wedding in normal circumstances, but in their case there was scant need for any of the normal fuss. Jennifer and Terry were coming down from London. Jennifer had confirmed to Heather that Race had asked her about her, 'but I didn't tell you because I didn't want to upset you.'

'You did the right thing,' Heather assured her.

'Just as you are doing now,' Jennifer commented. They were both in the room they had shared as girls, Jennifer had arrived just before lunch, and at three o'clock Heather was going to become Mrs Race Williams. 'Mum told me she felt guilty because she let Race see you,' Jennifer continued. 'She's worried that you might be marrying him against your will.'

'Not against my will: rather against my better judgment,' Heather said wryly, adding inconsequentially, 'Neil's taking it very badly.'

'He'll get over it,' Jennifer assured her cheerfully, with sisterly hard-heartedness, 'and it's better this way. I honestly believe he'd practically convinced himself that the baby was his. I gather he and Race didn't hit it off too well?'

'Not really,' Heather admitted. 'Neil's going away almost immediately after the wedding—to Switzerland, to do some photography. A group of them are going.' She thought of Sue Reynolds from the camera shop; she was going too. Perhaps Neil would find solace with her. She hoped so.

Heather had chosen to wear a simple cream dress for the ceremony. Nothing could hide her pregnancy, and she didn't intend to try. The baby was due in just over three months, and she prayed as she walked down the aisle on her uncle's arm that she was doing the right thing. Race was waiting for her, tall and dark, virtually a stranger; and fear coiled round her heart as she thought of how arid her life could turn out to be. Race could and would seek consolation elsewhere if need be, but what about her? Knowing how much she loved him, Heather knew it was impossible for her to find love with anyone else.

She would just have to gamble on the child she carried bringing them closer together. After all, as Race had told her only last night, they were sexually compatible and he had no intention of their marriage being merely a paper one.

'But what about love?' she had said huskily, and just for a moment a spasm of pain had crossed his face as though he too were putting aside old dreams.

Then he said, mockingly, 'We shall have to make do with our love for our child, won't we?'

They were going away for a brief 'honeymoon'. Heather hadn't wanted to, but Race had insisted. He needed a holiday, he had told her coolly, and this was the time of year when he always visited his villa in the Cayman Islands. 'We'll cut it short this time—stay a fortnight instead of a month.' He had also insisted on accompanying her on her hospital check-up, something she had always refused to let Neil do, and had questioned the doctor closely about any dangers there might be in her flying.

He had spent three days with her before the wedding, taking her out, talking to her about his plans for the future, and she had learned that he only intended to stay with the television company for a year. 'I want to concentrate more on my writing,' he had told her as they drove along the narrow Cotswold roads, 'but you needn't worry that we might be facing penury; I have several other directorships.'

It had been on that drive that Heather had seen the house. She had been map-reading and they had lost their way, taking a wrong turning and finding themselves on a winding country road, bordered by stone walls over which they could see glimpses of fields. The house was slightly set back from the road, Elizabethan and neglected, a battered 'For Sale' board outside. Perhaps it had something to do with her pregnancy, Heather didn't know, but she had been consumed with a desire to restore it to what it had once been, to lavish love and care on it and bring it back to life. Her aunt had been right when she had said that she was born to be a wife and mother. She didn't miss her London life in the slightest. Some women needed the challenge of a career, some had a creative urge they needed to fulfil, but Heather knew her desires would always be rooted in her home and family.

She had found herself thinking about the house when they returned to her aunt and uncle's, wondering if she hadn't married Race whether she could have afforded to buy it. Probably not. But London wasn't the place to bring up a child, not to her. She wanted her child to experience the same country childhood she had loved.

The cold presence of Race's ring as he slid it over her finger brought her back to the present. Her heart thudded. It was over, they were man and wife. The church bells pealed, music filling and swelling inside the small church. Heather noticed that her aunt was crying as she walked back down the aisle on Race's arm. She felt the baby kick and wanted to laugh.

'That's the first time I've seen you smile properly all week.' She glanced at Race, surprised to see how grim he looked—but then it couldn't have been easy for him either. At least *she* loved *him*; he had nothing apart from his sense of responsibility towards their child. As they stepped out into the sunshine a shiver of fear went through her. Had she done the right thing? Only time would tell.

CHAPTER NINE

As there was no direct flight from London to the Cayman Islands they were flying from Heathrow to the Caribbean and then taking the inter-island flight to the island where Race had his villa. The island was one of the smaller ones, he told her as they boarded their flight at Terminal 3, St James's, and one of the delights of the Caymans was that because of their relative inaccessibility they were still largely unspoiled.

'There isn't even a hotel on the island, although there are plans to build a marina. I've often fancied buying an ocean-going yacht myself. Perhaps if we have a son I shall.'

'A daughter could be equally interested in sailing,' Heather told him coolly. She wasn't sure how she felt as yet about the proprietorial attitude Race had adopted towards the baby. She had got used to thinking of the baby as hers, but Race was making it plain that he meant to have at least an equal say in anything to do with its future and upbringing. Could they make their marriage work? Heather wasn't naïve, and when Race had said they were sexually compatible she had been forced to admit that he was telling the truth. She was also forced to concede that he was right when he said that marriages succeeded with less, and that much could be accomplished by willingness and determination.

'Make no mistake, Heather,' he had told her the night before they married, 'I fully intend that our marriage will last. I don't go along with this idea that we owe it to ourselves to squeeze as much self-indulgent pleasure out of life as we can—not where children are concerned. They don't ask to be born, and we owe them a responsibility I'm not prepared to duck out of. I'll do my damnedest to make this marriage work and I expect the same sort of commitment from you. You must want the child, otherwise you'd have had an abortion; what you need to ask yourself now is, do you want it enough to make the sacrifices you'll have to make?'

Did she? Heather didn't know, all she did know was that badly as she wanted Race's child, she wanted Race more. The reasons behind her acceptance of his proposal were extremely complex, but the strongest single factor must surely have been the way she felt about it. That alone might not have been strong enough to make her marry him, but it had been there, unacknowledged when she made her decision.

'Tired?' The question was one any man might have asked his wife; brief and yet concerned, and the stewardess watched with understanding compassion as Heather shook her head. They had a long flight ahead of them, and even now she wasn't sure she wanted to go. Race had said they both needed the break, and she wondered if he was thinking of the stir her pregnancy was likely to cause among his friends and acquaintances. Men like Race did not get their women friends pregnant by accident, nor did they rush to marry them if they did. They had 'live-in' lovers, and meaningful relationships, and her condition was bound to result in a certain amount of speculation. There might even be those who might judge that she had deliberately become pregnant to force Race's hand. . . . Heather sighed.

'You *are* tired.' It was more of an accusation than a comment, and she shook her head again. She was too keyed up to be tired. They had spent the night at Race's London flat; a large, expensive apartment which, in spite of its expensive furnishings, Heather had found cold and cheerless. It was a bachelor's apartment, a show-place, and she could never visualise it as a home. 'We've got a long flight ahead of us, why don't you try and get some sleep?'

It was easier said than done. Heather had never been particularly keen on flying and the week had taken its toll on her. Her body wanted to sleep, wanted to return to that drowsy, satisfied state it had been in before Race reappeared in her life, but her mind wouldn't let it. She had slept in the guest room of Race's apartment, feeling more like an intruder than a wife. She knew that he was only marrying her because of the baby, but somehow after saying they were sexually compatible she hadn't expected him to let her sleep alone.

Perhaps her pregnant body repelled him. She knew that some were affected like that, but there had been no revulsion in the way he had touched and kissed her in the garden of her aunt's and uncle's home.

She tried to relax in her seat. They were travelling first-class and had ample room, but somehow her body felt heavy and uncomfortable. Perhaps their child objected to flight as much as she did, she reflected wryly as she turned away from Race and tried to court sleep. It was obvious that he didn't want to talk to her. He had some papers spread out in front of him and was frowning over them, her presence apparently forgotten.

Eventually she dozed off, only to be woken by the stewardess when she brought their lunch. Heather ate unenthusiastically, feeling heavy-eyed and dull. She refused any wine, thinking sardonically that had she always been so abstemious she might not be in the position she now was—or was she deluding herself? Would she have ended up in Race's arms anyway?

After lunch she slept again, losing interest in the film, and woke later in the afternoon to find that Race had pushed up the arm rest between them and that she was lying with her head on his shoulder, his arm supporting her.

'You might have been asleep,' he told her lazily as she opened her eyes, 'but Junior's been extremely active.' His fingers splayed possessively across the tautness of her stomach, warmth radiating into her body from them, and she watched him registering the movements of the baby's limbs, his harsh features softened to something approaching tenderness.

'Seems like he's practising to be a footballer,' he commented as she pulled away, hating herself for the completely unmaternal response of her body to his touch.

'And as I keep telling you, he could easily be a "she". Do you particularly want a boy?' she asked curiously.

He shook his head. 'I don't mind either way, as long as you're both healthy. I thought it would do you good to get away for a while, but now I'm not so sure that such a long flight was a good idea. Still, it won't be long now.'

Heather had an opportunity to stretch her legs when they put down at Barbados. The evening was full of the scents and sounds of the Caribbean, lush and tropical, and her skin was dewed with perspiration as the heat struck it, intensified by the cool, pressurised atmosphere of the plane.

She only just managed not to flinch when she saw the small plane which would transport them to St James's. Race frowned when he saw her reaction, and she bit her lip, thinking that he was probably regretting bringing her. Race was the last person to understand or be patient with fear. It was something he had probably never experienced in his life, she thought acidly.

In the event, perhaps because she was so tired, the flight wasn't the ordeal she had anticipated. It was too dark for her to see St James's as they came in to land, and after a mercifully brief delay Race had installed her and their luggage in a comfortably padded jeep which he told her was the most common form of transport on the island. 'With only one main road anything else is a waste of time,' he told her as he climbed in beside her and started the engine.

Heather was too tired to pay much attention to their surroundings as they drove away from the airport. She was aware of a small town clustering round the harbour and the odd light illuminating bungalows and villas dotted through the countryside, which was lushly green and fertile, Race told her as he drove skilfully along the rutted road.

Heather felt as though every bone in her body was aching when he eventually stopped in front of a neat villa, pink-washed in the lights of the jeep, the sound of the surf the only thing to break the silence, as he climbed out and walked towards the door.

'Stay there,' he commanded tersely when he saw she was going to follow him, and then he disappeared inside, light flooding through the windows. He was back within seconds, opening her door and lifting her up as easily as though she weighed no more than a feather. As a teenager she had often dreamed of being held like this, knowing it to be a very forlorn wish for a girl of her height, and yet here she was in Race's arms, his heart thudding slowly beneath her cheek.

The villa was two-storied and Race took her upstairs, kicking open a door and using his elbow to switch on the light as he carried her inside. 'Bed for you,' he told her, adding curtly when she protested that there was their luggage to unpack and a meal to make, 'You're exhausted, Heather. I can easily unpack and make us a meal, always supposing you can stay awake long enough to eat it.'

The large double bed looked extremely inviting, the curtains billowing slightly in the evening breeze wafting through the open window. Race had turned on the air-conditioning as he walked in and the muggy heat she had experienced on the drive from the airport was gradually disappearing.

'Race, I can't go to bed yet,' she protested half-heartedly, 'I want to have a shower—change my clothes. . . .'

'I'll bring your case up for you, but in the meantime you can rest. It will take half an hour or so to heat up the water. No, Heather,' he said firmly, sensing the protests hovering on her lips. 'I'm your husband now,' he reminded her.

'Which doesn't give you the right to tell me what to do,' Heather objected spiritedly.

'No,' he agreed softly, 'but it does give me the right to do this.' As he lowered her towards the bed, his lips brushed lightly across hers, the contact so tantalising that Heather wasn't even aware of the mattress beneath her until Race withdrew his arms to place his palms flat on the bed either side of her, his mouth continuing to explore the shape of hers, his tongue stroking along the outline of her lips until she felt fluid and pliant beneath it, her eyes closing in heated pleasure as his teeth nipped gently at the fullness of her bottom lip, teasing it until she moaned a small protest and locked her arms round his neck, her fingers delving into the thick darkness of his hair, pleading with him to deepen the kiss.

To her chagrin Heather felt him withdraw, his fingers unlocking hers and placing them gently at her side. 'I've got to unpack, remember?' Was it just her imagination, or was there a hint of taunting mockery in his voice? Could he have guessed how she felt about him?

Shivering, Heather withdrew. That was something she could not bear. He was being considerate and tender with her because she carried his child, but he didn't want her love and she was deceiving herself if she thought otherwise.

She fell asleep almost immediately, and woke much later to find herself alone and faintly chilled. Race had been as good as his word, she saw, because her empty case lay by the window and on the chair was a clean nightdress. He had warned her to buy cotton underwear to wear while they were away, because of the heat, and the nightdress looked oddly demure with its sprigs of flowers and dainty broderie anglaise bodice fastened with soft apricot ribbons.

She glanced at her watch, which she hadn't altered from Greenwich Mean Time, and wondered hazily what time it was. It was still dark, and the house seemed silent. She went downstairs and found Race in the study engrossed in some paperwork.

'I thought this was supposed to be a holiday—for both of us,' she chided him when he looked up.

'I thought I'd let you sleep—and you shouldn't object, wifely duty though it may be—after all, it keeps me from your bed,' he jeered, 'but on this occasion not for long. The villa has two bedrooms, but only one is furnished, and I'll be damned if I'll sleep downstairs.'

If he knew the villa possessed only one bed, why had he brought her here, since he plainly didn't want to share it with her? Heather wondered with an unusual snap of temper, but she didn't say anything.

She explored the villa on her own and discovered a large and pleasant living room, with huge patio doors which opened onto a secluded courtyard. The only other room was a good-sized family kitchen, with enough space for a table and chairs. The units were spankingly modern, the floor, like all the other floors in the villa tiled, for coolness and cleanliness.

'Will the water be hot by now?' she asked Race when she took him a cup of coffee. Her body felt grubby and sticky from the flight, and she was longing for a shower.

'Should be, you've been asleep for four hours.' He saw her expression and laughed mockingly. 'I told you you were tired.'

The bathroom was blissfully modern and Heather stayed under the shower longer than she had anticipated, enjoying the cool spray of the water against her skin. There was a full-length mirror on one wall and she studied herself with the objectivity she had learned as a model, wondering why she found such intense pleasure in knowing it was Race's child she nurtured inside her.

She smiled as she touched her skin, glowing and fresh after her shower, her breasts full, the nipples darker than they had been, a woman's body and not a girl's. If only Race loved her the way she loved him, how perfect these months would be as they shared together the wonder of making a new life! Some women delighted in pregnancy because they were natural mothers, unfulfilled without a child, but Heather knew her intense pleasure sprang more from the fact that the baby was the living proof of how she felt about Race; an elemental, fiercely female need for the fulfilment of feeling her body ripen with the fertile seed of her lover; a thing apart from simply wanting a child, something that nature had instilled in women at the dawn of time as a safeguard against the dying out of the race, something which still persisted against all the laws of logic or modern-day sophistication. A sense of completeness that knowing their lovemaking had resulted in a baby brought her.

Shaking her head over the complexity of her thoughts, Heather was surprised to discover that she was crying, her cheeks wet with tears. She was just going to wipe them away when the bathroom door opened inwards and Race walked in, his forehead furrowed in a frown of concern.

'Heather, are you. . . .' He broke off when he saw her, and Heather was suddenly acutely conscious of her nakedness. It was one thing for her to admire and take pleasure in the way her body bloomed with the baby, but Race was hardly likely to feel the same way.

'You're crying.' It was an accusation, edged with anger. 'Why? Because you didn't marry that cousin of yours? Because it isn't his baby you're carrying? Heather, for God's sake, don't!' he groaned as her tears fell faster, motivated by she knew not what emotion, unless it was the sheer pain of loving him and knowing her love was not returned. 'Heather. . . .' His arms locked round her, his lips moved softly over her skin as his tongue caught up the damp salt of her tears. 'You're so very beautiful like this,' he told her huskily, his voice thickening with emotion, 'so very, very beautiful.'

He bent his head to her breast, gently caressing the tender flesh, his fingers cupping her roundness tenderly, as she quivered and tensed, feeling her body's unmistakable reaction to him as his hand stroked slowly downwards, exploring her burgeoning shape, his lips warm against her breast. But there was no passion in his touch, Heather thought achingly, none of the desire and wanting she could feel within her.

'Race,' she protested unsteadily, longing to tell him how she felt, how much she longed for him to kiss her, to possess her as he had done before, but his head lifted from her breast, his lips stroking gently across her skin.

'Hush, it's all right,' he said quietly, 'I'm not going to hurt you. It's just that it's a pretty stupendous feeling knowing that's my child inside you. Come on, I'll help you on with this.'

He picked up her nightdress, dropping it over her head as though she were a child, firmly securing the ribbons when she had slipped her arms into the sleeves, no trace of the desire he had felt once towards her in the grey eyes that surveyed her slowly when he had finished. Heather felt then that her last frail hope had died. She had thought they might build something from their marriage based on the desire she knew he had felt for her, but it seemed she was to be denied even that. All that Race wanted from her was his child, and for her pride's sake she would be wise to remember that.

She woke once during the night and felt the warm bulk of his body behind her, knowing a longing to turn into his arms but repressing it, only to find in the morning that she must have given in to it, because she woke to find herself curled up against him, his hand resting possessively on her stomach, the baby kicking enthusiastically against it. She thought he was asleep until she saw the glitter of grey between the narrowed lids, and a look of torment suddenly crossed his face as he said hoarsely, 'Dear God, Heather, why did this have to happen?'

Quickly pulling back the blankets, he thrust his legs on to the floor while she blinked rapidly to hide the

tears threatening to fall, hating herself for the agony
the anguish she heard in his voice caused her. She
already knew he had only married her because of the
baby, because of his scruples, so why should she feel
so hurt because he had just reinforced that knowledge?

The days merged one into the other. The villa had a
small private beach and Heather was able to sunbathe
without feeling uncomfortable. Race had brought
work with him and during the mornings she learned to
leave him alone while the distant sound of the
typewriter reached her through the open windows.
One of the local women came in to cook and clean.
She was fat and jolly and chuckled loudly when she
saw Heather. 'You make one very fine baby,' she told
Race, and Heather was amused to see a faint tinge of
colour darkening her husband's cheekbones. Race
embarrassed! She'd never thought she'd live to see the
day.

In the afternoons Race scuba-dived or swam,
Heather sometimes joining him to paddle leisurely in
the aquamarine seas, but feeling too pleasurably lazy
to exert herself to any great degree. The nights were
the hardest of all, when she had to try to sleep with
Race beside her, so close to him and yet really so very
far apart. What was physical intimacy without the
mental harmony to enrich and enhance it?

'Why don't you take your top off?' She hadn't heard
Race approach and sat up quickly putting down the
book she had been reading, her face colouring.

'The beach is perfectly private,' Race pointed out,
'and it doesn't look particularly comfortable. The
fabric is cutting into your skin.' He frowned, and
Heather told herself she was being ridiculously
imaginative for thinking that the thought displeased
him. It was true, though, that the bikini top she was

wearing was uncomfortable. Even in the week that they had been there her body had changed, and she couldn't deny that it would be pleasurable to feel the warmth of the sun and the cool tang of the on-shore breeze on her skin.

'I won't look, if that's what's troubling you,' Race said harshly. 'I wonder if you'd be as shy with your precious cousin? Was that why you left home, Heather? Because you knew he wanted you and that your aunt and uncle wouldn't approve? Was he the one you were thinking of when I made love to you? He wants you so badly he'd almost convinced himself that was his child inside you. . . .'

'Neil is my cousin, Race,' Heather protested, feeling her stomach muscles curl in protest at the anger she could sense within him. 'I had no idea how he felt. We were always good friends, but . . . .'

'You didn't know he desired you? And if you had known, Heather, what then?' he taunted. 'Would he have been the one to hear your virgin cries of pleasure? To impregnate your body with his child?'

Why was he talking to her like this? He couldn't possibly be jealous of Neil. Or was it simply that he resented the fact that Neil had known about the baby when he did not?

'I had no idea about Neil,' she told him shakily. 'And I left home because I'd . . . because I'd had a bad experience with someone else. Someone I thought loved me, but who in the event merely wanted to marry me because my parents had left me some money. I wasn't a particularly popular teenager; being so tall made me feel awkward and unsure of myself. When Brad took an interest in me, I put him up on a pedestal. Neil helped me to find self-confidence. He was the one who suggested I take up modelling; he's always been a keen photographer.'

'Don't I know it!' Race grated savagely. 'He photographed my wife, pregnant with my child . . . God, Heather, can't you imagine what it did to me to see that picture, to open a local newspaper and see you staring back at me, then, when I'd.· . . .'

'Forgotten all about me?' Heather supplied sweetly. 'I expect it was quite a shock. Race . . . Race, where are you going?' she asked curiously as he turned his back one her and strode back to the villa.

'To get myself·a drink,' he snarled back at her. 'I damn well need one!'

To help him forget that he was trapped. in their marriage? Heather wondered helplessly when he had gone. What on earth had made her talk to Race about Brad? She couldn't understand why she had confided in him. That had been her secret, something she hid away from everyone else. . . .

Race was right about one thing, though, she decided in irritation, seconds later. Her bikini top was uncomfortable, and since he had gone back to work and she could hear the angry rattle of his typewriter, she felt perfectly safe in removing it.

The balm of the sun against her bare skin made her stretch languorously, her book forgotten as she felt a familiar drowsiness steal over her. She really was growing lazy, sleeping like this every afternoon, but it was undeniably pleasant to let her body relax, her mind drift.

She woke up to find Race standing over her carrying a tray of tea. 'I thought you might like a drink.'

Whatever had made him angry seemed to have disappeared, but Heather flushed as she felt his glance linger on the pale curves of her breasts. Did he find her ugly with her body heavy with pregnancy? She wanted to reach for her top but felt awkward about doing so, not wanting Race to guess how much his proximity affected her, and said instead, 'I'd better go inside and get some sun-cream. I don't want to burn.'

'There's some here,' Race told her, picking up a tube she had forgotten. Turn over and I'll do it for you.'

Hoping her expression hadn't given her away, Heather dutifully rolled on to her side. The cream felt cool on the back of her thighs, the long, stroking movement of Race's fingers dangerously arousing. Her relief when he moved to the outside of her thighs was short-lived when she felt him untie the bow that held her bikini bottom in place, his fingers stroking up along the curve of her hip and then round to the fullness of her stomach, gently massaging the taut skin until she had to close her eyes in dizzy protest, willing herself not to utter the small groan of pleasure she could feel building up inside her.

'What's the matter?' The movement of his hand stopped and she opened her eyes to find him watching her closely. 'You've gone quite pale. Are you feeling all right? I wasn't hurting you, was I?'

What could she say? 'Junior seemed to enjoy it,' she joked weakly, 'I think he's gone to sleep.'

'I'm glad I can please one member of my family.' His voice was so dry Heather thought she must have imagined the fleeting glance of pain in his eyes. Was he, too, wondering what it would be like if there was love between them, if she was the woman who held his heart?

'Don't get up yet, we haven't finished.' He squeezed some more cream on to his hands and smoothed them softly against her breasts, cupping them with his palms, the sensation utterably pleasurable, as his fingers moved delicately over the pale flesh.

'Heather.' He said her name harshly, alerting her drowsing senses to alarm, a sweetly painful gasp wrung from her lips as his thumb stroked slowly over her nipple, his face oddly pale as he stared down at her. His eyes closed in a sudden gesture of defeat as he placed his mouth against the hollow between her breasts, his breathing harshly ragged, as he muttered something she couldn't hear before letting his lips close over the nipple he had been stroking, tugging gently on the puckered flesh until it flowered against his tongue and a fierce wave of heat consumed her, her body tensing in remembered pleasure.

'Heather.' His voice sounded thick, almost unrecognisable, 'God forgive me, I shouldn't have done that. I. . . .' He raked his fingers through her hair, sitting down beside her. 'I just found the sight of you unutterably arousing, I guess. When . . . when the baby comes, do you . . . will you . . . Are you going to breast-feed it?' he asked sombrely, and Heather felt her skin colour as she realised the direction of his thoughts and felt her own undeniable response to them.

'I . . . I don't know.' It was a lie. How often already had she longed impatiently to hold the baby in her arms, feeling it draw strength and succour from her body?

'If you don't you'll be depriving it of a very special bond,' he said huskily, adding stupefyingly, 'And if you do, no doubt I'll be as jealous as hell.'

And with that he got up and walked back to the villa, leaving Heather trying to come to terms with her disordered thoughts, the tea he had brought her growing cold in the pot.

They returned to Heathrow five days later, and drove straight to the apartment, which was every bit as unwelcoming as Heather had remembered. She didn't see Race until dinner time, as he had been up early and had left straight after breakfast. Although their holiday had relaxed her physically, mentally she was still keyed up, and Race didn't seem to have gained any benefit at all from their break. He looked tired, and almost drained, she thought as she studied him across the table.

'I have to go out after dinner,' he told her curtly when he had finished his meal. 'By the way, I've got something for you. A belated wedding present which isn't quite ready yet.'

He tossed her an envelope and Heather opened it curiously, wondering what on earth it could be. A wedding present wasn't something she had expected. After all, their marriage was scarcely the type that demanded one. Her gasp of surprise as she slid the papers from the envelope caused Race to lift his head, but she was too engrossed in what she was studying to notice.

'It's the house,' she said slowly at last. 'The Elizabethan house we saw. . . . But Race, you never said . . . how did you know . . .?'

'I saw the way you looked at it,' he said simply, 'and this apartment is no place to bring up a family. And by a family I don't just mean one child,' he warned her hardily. 'The legal formalities for the house will be completed by the end of next week. 'It's basically sound, but one hell of a lot needs doing to it. If you don't feel up to it, hire a firm of interior decorators.'

'Oh no!' the protest was out before she could stop it. 'I'd rather do it myself, really, Race,' she said slowly. 'I know it will take longer; we might just about have it finished before his first birthday,' she said lightly, touching her stomach, 'but if you've no objections I'd prefer it that way.'

'Suit yourself.' He shrugged broad shoulders encased in the smoothly expensive fabric of his suit.

'I'd better get a move on. Don't wait up for me, and Heather. . . .' She turned to look at him. 'When you're making your arrangements, remember that the master suite will be occupied by both of us, won't you?'

So he did still desire her, Heather thought dazedly when he had gone and she had read and re-read the details sheet of the house. Or was it simply that he wanted to reinforce the image of a compact family unit? Did he think she might turn to someone else if he neglected her, Neil maybe, and so jeopardise their children's security?

Only one thing was clear, and that was that she would never know the motivation behind his actions unless she asked him, and she was scarcely likely to do that. He had bought her the house, had recognised her unexpressed desire for it and had given it to her. Surely that proved something? She fell asleep feeling much happier than she had done for some time, but her happiness disappeared the following morning when she saw a photograph of Race and a familiar, tiny blonde adorning the gossip column of her newspaper.

'Entrepreneur Race Williams and Lady Davinia Fane dining together at the new restaurant, Raffles, opened by TV personality John Richards,' the caption read, and Heather felt her happiness turn to bitterness. Was the house Race's way of buying her off, burying her in the country while he was free to live a bachelor life in the city? She could almost laugh aloud at her naïveté.

Telling herself that it was pointless to brood, she rang her aunt to tell her about the house. 'Yes, I know, darling,' she heard Lydia say. 'Race asked your uncle to see to it all for him. I think he would have asked Neil, but poor Neil's been so touchy about your marriage! However, he seems to be getting over things

now. We had a card from him the other day, he's
decided to stay on for another couple of weeks in
Switzerland, and so has Sue Reynolds. When are you
coming down?' she asked eventually. 'I'm longing to
see you.'

'Once the house is legally ours. I'd like to move in
before the baby comes if possible, but there's an awful
lot of work to be done.'

This was a view Jennifer reinforced when she called
to see her later that day.

'I've got the day off,' she told Heather in response
to her query. 'Goodness, you're looking well—unlike
your new lord and master, who looks positively
frazzled! His temper isn't too sweet either, fatherhood
is obviously proving burdensome to him. Oh, Heather,
I didn't mean it that way,' she apologised hurriedly
when she saw her cousin's face. 'Oh, God, this tactless
tongue of mine!'

'It's all right,' Heather assured her wryly. 'Let's not
have any pretence between us, Jen, it's hard enough
pretending to anyone else. Race married me because of
the baby—that and because of the circumstances of his
own childhood.'

'But he must care something about you, Heather,
and you love *him*.'

Heather shook her head, and showed her cousin
the newspaper. 'I do love him, Jen,' she agreed
quietly, 'but I'm not going to fall into the trap of
thinking everything's going to be happy ever after.
Now, tell me about Terry and your plans,' she
charged, deftly changing the subject.

CHAPTER TEN

'Oh, Heather, it's gorgeous!' Jennifer pronounced half-enviously. 'I can't get over the amount you've done since you first got the house. How have you done it?'

'I haven't got anything else to do,' Heather reminded her cousin wryly as they headed back to the top of the stairs. Her cousin's praise had been heart-warming, all the more so as Race hadn't made any comment at all when he had come down the previous weekend. The house was by no means finished, but she had done as much as she intended for the moment. With the baby's birth barely a month away she knew it would be foolish to overtire herself.

'When do you actually move in?' Jennifer asked her when they were back downstairs, drinking mugs of coffee in the attractive farmhouse-style kitchen that Heather had had completely gutted and then re-fitted by a sympathetic local craftsman who had understood and appreciated her desire to combine the best of everything that was modern in function with a design that would complement the exposed beams and brickwork of the kitchen. The effect was all that Heather had hoped for. The kitchen was supremely functional and yet had all the warmth and charm of a children's storybook illustration, right down to the huge tabby cat snoozing on one of the chairs.

'Straight away,' Heather told her. 'I've been living here for the past week, and now that the workmen have gone there's nothing to stop us moving in properly.'

'Umm, Mum's been worried about you staying here

by yourself, and I can understand why. You *are* a bit remote, Heather.'

'I have a car and a telephone,' Heather reminded her dryly, wishing it was her husband who was expressing such concern for her well-being rather than her cousin.

'But Race will be here with you from now on?' Jennifer queried anxiously.

'Oh, yes,' Heather assured her airily, not daring to look at her in case she read her own doubt in her eyes. Apart from staying the odd weekend at the house Race had continued to live in the London apartment. He had offered no explanation for this and Heather had not asked for one, not after she had seen that item in the gossip column.

Her mouth compressed slightly. When Race had talked about their marriage, she had imagined naïvely that fidelity was part of the package; at least initially, while they tried to make things work. But it seemed she was mistaken.

No wonder he had bought her this house! She swallowed on the pain tensing her throat, not wanting Jennifer to guess how miserable she felt. Now, with the work on the house completed for the moment, she had nothing to do but sit down and wait for the baby; and of course to worry about the wisdom of marrying Race.

The master bedroom had been prepared as he had instructed, for them to share, but so far she had slept alone in the huge fourposter bed which complemented the period of the house. Off the bedroom was a brand-new bathroom plus a small dressing-room lined with cupboards and wardrobes, and large enough to take the baby's things for the first few months, until he or she was old enough to sleep in the small nursery she had taken such pains with.

'You know that Neil's still going out with Sue, don't you?' Jennifer asked when they had finished their coffee. 'Any regrets?'

'No.' Surprisingly, it was true. Race might not love her, but she did love him and she could never have married Neil.

'Rich is coming home for Christmas,' Jen continued. 'Mum's thrilled to bits. She wants you and Race to come for dinner Christmas Day.'

'I'd love to,' Heather told her, 'but I'm not sure what Race's plans are.' Christmas was still five months away, but Heather well knew her aunt's habit of organising things early. Jennifer wrinkled her nose.

'Umm, I know. Terry was all for us spending Christmas in Switzerland, but I've managed to change his mind.'

'Have you set a date yet?' Heather asked her cousin, listening sympathetically while Jennifer listed the difficulties of finding a suitable house close to the centre of London.

'Once we find somewhere we'll probably get married almost straight away. I'll have to be going soon,' she added, glancing at her watch. 'Sure you'll be okay?'

'Race is coming down tomorrow,' Heather reassured her. He had rung her only that morning to warn her of his visit. Heather's mouth twisted. It hurt her to think that Race considered himself a visitor in what should have been their home.

He arrived just as Heather was hanging out some washing. She had taken advantage of the good weather to wash a pile of new nappies which had been delivered that morning. The van had trundled down the drive just as she was finishing breakfast, and when he saw that she was on her own the driver had cheerfully carried the crib and other equipment upstairs for her. Heather had ordered them from the same shop where Neil had ordered the pram which now stood in stately splendour in the hall, totally impractical in many ways, and yet she hadn't been able to resist giving it a trial push enjoying its expensively cushioned bounce. Dear Neil, she was so glad that he seemed to have found happiness with Sue.

'Very domesticated,' drawled Race when she had finished. 'Workmen all gone?'

'Yes, everything's finished for the time being. What do you intend to do about the London apartment?' she asked him as they walked back to the house. Her movements had slowed and Race had to adjust his pace to match hers, his glance taking in her tousled hair and smooth tanned skin. Heather flushed, suddenly selfconscious. What a fright she must look, her hair all untidy, bulging all over the place, no proper make-up on! No wonder he preferred to stay in London.

'Nothing for the time being,'

Heather's heart sank. So she had been right. He did intend to stay in London. Was he regretting their marriage to that extent already? His next words surprised, so at variance with her thoughts that she half-stumbled against him, welcoming the sudden protective grip of his arm as he balanced her.

'Mrs Dunn will keep an eye on it for me, and then after the baby's birth we'll decide what to do with it.'

'You mean you're going to stay down here?' She asked the question cautiously, not daring to let herself hope too much.

Race frowned, and she wondered painfully if he was thinking about Davinia and the fact that staying with her would mean he could see less of her.

'It is our home,' he pointed out coolly, 'and you're too near to the baby's birth to be left alone.'

Disappointment and misery fired her anger. 'If that's all that's worrying you I could always go and stay with my aunt and uncle.'

They were in the hall and Race said sharply, 'No . . . damn!' He swore suddenly as he bumped into the pram. 'What the . . .'

'Neil bought it for me,' Heather said quickly, flushing as she remembered their day in Gloucester and seeing Race. That must have been the day he went to ask the newspaper offices where he could find Neil.

'Race . . . Race, what are you doing?' she asked him as he lifted the label off the pram and picked up the phone, angrily punching in the numbers.

'Sending this back,' he grated at her. 'I'm not having him buying things for my child, cousin or no cousin!'

Heather was stunned. Why was he so angry? Neil had bought her the pram as a gift, and although she had thought he had been too extravagant she had not wanted to hurt his feelings by returning it.

'Race, I wish you hadn't done that,' she protested tremulously when he had instructed the shop to collect the pram. 'Neil will be so hurt. . . .'

'Damn Neil!' he swore forcefully, slamming down the receiver. 'What about me, Heather?' he demanded bitterly. 'Don't my feelings count?' His mouth compressed. 'But we both know the answer to that, don't we? Dear God, I wish I'd never . . .'

His eyes went to the bulge of her stomach and Heather felt as though she were going to faint. She wanted to hate him for making his resentment so plain, but somehow she couldn't.

'I do understand how you feel, Race,' she said huskily, 'and I promise you I'll do my best to make it as easy as possible for you.'

'Do you?' he asked thickly as he strode towards the

stairs. 'That's bloody generous of you, Heather . . . but save it, will you? It isn't generosity I want from you.'

No, it was his freedom, Heather thought unhappily as she watched him walk lithely up the stairs. He opened the door to their room and she paused, not knowing whether to go after him or leave him. In the end she opted for the latter.

Race stayed for ten days, during which they treated one another like polite strangers. The pram disappeared to be replaced by one which was even more magnificent and obviously expensive, and Heather eyed it with increasing revulsion. If she had thought that sharing the intimacy of the fourposter bed would improve matters between them she had been wrong. Race normally worked in the evenings, coming to bed long after she was asleep. Her pregnancy made her feel more tired than usual and she slept more deeply. Had more bedrooms been ready, Heather suspected Race would have suggested that they slept separately. But it had been on his instructions that she had prepared this room. Had he decided after all that the duty he felt he owed his unborn child was not as strong as he had first imagined? Heather had no way of knowing.

On the eleventh day after his arrival the phone rang, and she heard him answer it in the sitting-room-cum-library which she had decorated with such care to make it both comfortable and practical from a working point of view. Yew bookcases lined one wall, and the desk she had chosen was large enough to house Race's typewriter and telephone. Hidden away in the cupboards below the bookshelves were the video and stereo equipment, and the Colefax and Fowler chintzes, with their soft yellow background and misty blue and grey flowers, filled the room with sunshine and warmth.

She heard his footsteps crossing the hall as he called her name. She had been in the kitchen preparing lunch, and when he found her he said curtly, 'I have to go to London on business. I'll only be away the one night. I should be back in time for dinner tomorrow.'

'I could go and stay with my aunt,' Heather suggested. She wasn't normally timid, but she didn't like the thought of being so completely alone.

'No . . . no, I want you to stay here,' Race said coldly. 'It's just not going to work, is it?' he added with bitter savagery. 'You won't let it, will you, Heather? How can it work when every time my back's turned you're running back to your precious cousin?'

Heather didn't try to defend herself. She couldn't understand what had prompted the attack although she knew that he resented Neil. Half an hour later she heard the sound of his car engine firing. She was standing in the kitchen, by the sink, her hands automatically going through the motions of washing her coffee mug as the tears coursed relentlessly down her face.

How long could they go on like this? Race obviously loathed and resented her. They had none of the closeness she had hoped they might find when they returned from the Caymans; the Race who had touched her so comfortingly and tenderly then might never have been, and she was finding it increasingly hard to believe that this cold, bitter man was the same one who had brought her body to such a pitch of pleasure that all she had desired was his possession of her.

She was in the kitchen trying to remove the net curtain from the window two days later, when she heard a car in the drive. She had woken up that morning consumed by an urge to spring-clean, and when Neil's face appeared in her line of vision she grinned down at him, calling out that the back door was open.

'Heather, what the hell do you think you're doing?' he called out anxiously behind her as he stepped into the kitchen. She was just reaching for the curtain, stretching out to grasp it when suddenly she started to overbalance. Neil caught her, his face contorted with anxiety as he helped her into a chair. 'Heather, for God's sake,' he protested hotly, 'you shouldn't be doing things like that! Where's Williams? Doesn't he care? He should be with you, here.'

'Race is in London on business, and I'm not an invalid, Neil,' Heather placated. 'Sit down and I'll make us both a cup of coffee.'

'No, you sit down! God, Heather, you nearly gave me a heart attack! What on earth were you doing?'

'Trying to get the curtain down to wash it,' Heather said mildly. 'Now you're here you can get it down for me. What brings you here, by the way?'

'Can't I even call and see you now?' His mouth compressed. 'I had a phone call this morning—about the pram.'

'Race wouldn't let me keep it,' Heather told him huskily, biting her lip as she remembered the scene the pram had occasioned. She winced suddenly, rubbing the base of her spine. Her back had been aching on and off all morning, the pain gradually increasing until it was now quite uncomfortable.

Neil made their coffee and handed Heather's to her, studying her gravely. 'Heather, are you happy?' he asked bluntly. 'I'm worried about you.'

'Yes, I am,' she lied, gasping suddenly at the pain that caught her off guard. Instantly Neil was at her side, his face grey and anxious. 'Heather. . . .'

'It's perfectly all right,' she told him, managing a small smile. 'Probably a false alarm, but if you could telephone your mother.' Strange that the first person she wanted was her aunt; well, not the first. Race was the first, but it was pointless trying to phone him, she didn't even know where he was.

An hour later her aunt was saying briskly, 'Well, if you want my opinion it's no false alarm. Hospital for you, my girl. Neil, you can drive us. I'll sit in the back with Heather.'

Of the three of them Neil was the most distressed, Heather thought lazily, trying to remember everything she had learned during her relaxation classes, monitoring her breathing and trying not to let anxiety feather down her spine when she realised how much closer together the pains were coming.

'You're all right,' her aunt assured her comfortably. 'Plenty of time yet. Neil, try to concentrate on the road,' she adjured her son, drawing an exchanged smile between Heather and the latter as their eyes met in the driving mirror.

It was all wrong, though, Heather thought unhappily half an hour later as she walked into the hospital, Neil supporting her on one side, her aunt on the other. Race was the one who should be with her. Race was the one she wanted, she thought, wincing beneath the onslaught of another pain.

'Come along, Mrs Williams,' the Sister said encouragingly. 'Everything's going to be fine.'

'Race,' she protested huskily as the nurse came to lead her away. 'Race. . . .'

'Don't worry, we'll get him here,' her aunt assured her. 'Neil's gone to ring Jenny now, and we'll leave a message at the flat. 'He'll be here, Heather, don't worry. You just concentrate on having this baby. . . .'

It was surprising that she still had the space to worry about Race, Heather thought tiredly, after what seemed like hours of pain and instruction.

'Everything's going fine, Mrs Williams,' the Sister assured her, wiping the perspiration from her forehead. 'You're going to have to start working hard quite soon. Are you quite comfortable?'

Heather managed to nod her head. 'My husband. . . .'

'Yes . . . yes. He'll be here,' she soothed. After that everything was a blur; Sister hadn't been exaggerating when she said she was going to have to work.

'Don't push yet, Mrs Williams,' she heard someone saying to her, and then an aside, her hearing was suddenly acute enough to hear as she added, 'She's getting overtired . . . I wish her husband would arrive. It would give her the encouragement she needs.'

'How's the heartbeat?' she heard someone else ask and suddenly she was consumed with fear, both for herself and her baby. She heard someone crying and it wasn't until she saw her aunt's anxious face that she realised it was herself.

'Race . . . I want Race. . . .' she gasped as she tried to fight against the tide of pain; against the knowledge that Race didn't care enough to be with her.

'Yes . . . yes . . . he's coming,' her aunt soothed her, and then there was more pain and desolation until suddenly she was aware of warm fingers curling round her hand, giving her strength, tenderness in the hand that wiped the sweat from her face. She opened her eyes. Race's grey ones, stricken with fear and anguish, looked back at her, immediately recognisable despite the mask and gown he was wearing.

'Oh, Race. . . .' Strangely, his anxiety helped to calm her.

'Come along, Mrs Williams,' the doctor boomed heartily at her side, 'this isn't the time to go all moony-eyed over your husband, you've got work to do. That's right, laddie,' she heard him saying to

Race, 'just keep helping her. Come along now, Mrs Williams . . . push . . . yes, that's it . . .!'

It was over, and she had done it, Heather thought beatifically. She had a son . . . a marvellous, perfect son, who bawled lustily until the nurse placed him against her body. Heather reached out to touch him wonderingly, amazed by the sturdy concentration of his unwinking baby gaze. Who said newborn babies couldn't focus? For a moment the nursing staff had moved away from the bed, taking with them the noise and bustle of the birth. Heather gazed at her son in awe, shaken by the wave of love that consumed her.

'Heather. . . .' She blinked absently and glanced up at Race. For a moment she had almost forgotten he was there. He reached down, touching the baby's face, examining the small fingers. 'I'm sorry I wasn't here. . . .' Surely those couldn't be tears she could see sparkling against his lashes?

Curiously she reached up, touching him, staring at the diamond drop that came away on her fingers. 'Dear God,' Race exhaled on a tortured breath. 'I couldn't even be here when you needed me the most. No, it was Neil who was there. Neil. . . .'

'Come along, Mr Williams,' the nurse interrupted cheerfully, 'we've got to get your wife and son tidied up now. You can come back later.'

'Heather's he's gorgeous, let me cuddle him again.'

Grinning, Heather handed her son over to her aunt. 'Umm . . . my first grandchild—well, we look on you as our daughter,' she told her niece affectionately, burying her face in the small chubby neck. 'Babies have a smell all of their own, don't they?'

'Yes,' Heather agreed, laughing, 'sick and . . .'

'Now, that's not what I meant,' her aunt chided.

'Heather,' she placed Robert Paul Williams in the cradle at Heather's side and continued seriously, 'darling, don't think I'm being interfering, but you know, motherhood is a wonderful and absorbing thing, sometimes so absorbing that we tend to forget that men don't always view parenthood as we do ourselves. . . .'

'You mean I mustn't neglect my husband?'

Heather frowned. How could she explain to her aunt that Race was the one who was neglecting her? He spent more and more time in London, coming home only at weekends, and this weekend he wasn't even doing that. He had told her last Sunday, when he left, not to expect him.

'Umm, well, I've said my piece,' her aunt told her, getting up, 'and I'll just add this one more thing. The birth of a child, especially a first child, can be a traumatic thing for both parents. Sometimes a man, a sensitive man, finds it hard to make the first physical overtures. Giving birth is hard work,' she added, 'watching someone give birth can be even harder. Men often don't realise how tough the female body actually is. What I'm trying to say,' she concluded frankly, 'is that Race may be staying away because he doesn't want to hurt you. He's probably frightened that if he stays he might . . .'

'Be overcome with passion for me?' Heather supplied, smiling lightly. If only that was the case! But she could hardly tell her aunt the truth; that she suspected Race was staying away for no better reason that that he was quite simply bored with her.

On Saturday afternoon she was just feeding Robert prior to his afternoon sleep when she heard a car drawing up outside. She had been resting herself, and it had hardly seemed necessary to change out of the fine lawn nightdress she was wearing to feed the baby.

She had recovered her figure completely, her stomach flat and taut once more, and she glanced down at her son's small head with its sprinkling of dark hair so like his father's with tender amusement as he sucked strongly on her breast. His cry of angry frustration as she eased him away made her laugh, but her laughter turned to a frown as she went to the window and realised that the car was Race's.

What was he doing here? Fear gnawed at her. Had he come for a showdown? To tell her that their marriage had been a mistake? She heard him climbing the stairs, calling her name.

'I'm in here, Race,' she called back, going to the door. Robert was still sleeping in the dressing room. There had seemed little point in transferring him to the nursery with Race away so much, and her face flushed as she remembered how, when she had planned the nursery, she had thought that Race would appreciate their privacy. How could his desire for her have gone so completely?

Perhaps because desire was like that, Heather reflected miserably; desire wasn't love, and once assuaged. . . .

'I wasn't expecting you this weekend.'

'No . . .'

Heather flushed as she realised that Race was looking at her breasts, until an angry wail from her son reminded her that he was still probably hungry.

'I was just feeding Robert,' she told him, huskily, expecting him to leave. 'I put him down when I heard the car. . . .'

'And he plainly resents it,' Race said dryly, walking round to the crib and picking up his son. How tiny Robert looked when Race held him, Heather thought, watching them, and yet in reality he was a large baby and very heavy. Now, with his small face screwed up and red with rage, he reminded Heather of an angry old man. Race walked towards her, still holding him, and the moment he came near her Robert stopped crying.

'He's got a one-track mind,' Race commented as the baby started to nuzzle him.

'An instinct for survival,' Heather told him, taking Robert in her own arms, and settling herself back in the rocker. She enjoyed these moments with her son, and after all the lectures she had received at the hospital about the benefits of breast-feeding it was strange to discover that the one thing they had not mentioned was the enormous pleasure she derived from the physical contact with her child. She looked up at Race, but he was standing with his back to her, staring out of the window, his hands in his pockets. The moment she sat down Robert started to nuzzle her greedily, his eyes closing in patent satisfaction as she gave him her nipple. As always the rapt expression on his face absorbed her, a wave of emotion engulfing her.

'Heather. . . .' She looked up to discover that Race had come to stand beside her, his voice jagged and raw as he stared down at the baby at her breast. Something in the sight seemed to affect him. Heather saw the muscle clench in his jaw, a dark film of colour stealing over his skin. 'Heather. . . .'

He stopped again as Robert released her, and then stared round-eyed up at him until Heather moved, and threatened with the removal of his lunch he started to suck with renewed hunger. Heather let him have his fill. The nurse had told her that it was impossible to over-feed a breast-fed baby, and certainly he seemed to be thriving. She heard Race move and the door close behind him. What was it about the sight of her feeding their child that had affected him so strongly? Was it because he resented her?

As she hadn't expected him home, she hadn't planned a large evening meal, but there was sufficient in the freezer for her not to need to worry. 'Don't bother with any of that,' Race told her when he walked in and found her busy. 'At least, not for me—I'm not hungry.'

He paced the kitchen impatiently, but didn't say anything, and Heather wondered why he had come. She herself didn't have much appetite, but she forced herself to eat the omelette she had prepared, watching Race quickly downing the large whisky he had poured himself. She hadn't touched alcohol since the commencement of her pregnancy, but now she felt the need for something to bolster her courage, and accepted the glass of wine he handed to her, slightly dismayed to discover how quickly it went to her head. The evening dragged by in silence. With virtually every breath Heather expected to hear Race saying that he wanted a divorce. When nothing had happened by ten o'clock she announced that she was going to bed. To her surprise, Race announced that he too was tired.

'I've decided to leave Southern earlier than I'd planned and I spent nearly all yesterday negotiating terms.' It was news to Heather that he was leaving the television company so soon. Why? Because he wanted to break all his existing ties? How far down the list was she? she wondered bitterly.

He was in bed when she returned from feeding Robert, propped up against the pillows, reading a magazine. His hair was still damp from his shower, tiny crops of moisture blistening on his body. A surge of love and need so great that it almost robbed her of breath swept over Heather. Dear God, how she loved him! She couldn't let him go. . . . But she would probably have to. But now, at this moment he was still her husband. . . .

Heather saw him glance at her briefly and then return to his magazine, piqued by his obvious lack of interest in her. The lamp beside the bed threw a warm glow across his skin, still richly tanned compared to hers. Almost without being aware of what she was doing Heather tugged at the bows securing the straps of her nightgown. The soft slither of it falling to the floor caught Race's attention and he looked up, his eyes dilating fractionally, the pupils enlarging as he looked at her. Without giving herself time to think, Heather walked towards him, reaching out to touch him with fingers that trembled, as she kneeled beside the bed.

'Heather?' She ignored the cautionary note in his voice, as her fingertips traced the hard bones of his shoulders, her lips exploring the warm curve of the one closest to her, tasting the salty male flesh, and feeling her body quiver in reaction. Race didn't touch her, but he hadn't rejected her either, she thought, growing bolder, her fingernails raking softly through the fine hairs arrowing downwards along his body, feeling him tense as she reached his navel. 'Heather. . . .'

She ignored the implicit command, tensing when his fingers clamped on her wrist, flattening her palm against the tautness of his belly. She felt his muscles clench, but before he could push her away she lowered her head, hoping he wouldn't see the fear and uncertainty in her eyes, and brushed her lips hypnotically against the flat, dark aureole of flesh, so different from her own fuller, more feminine nipples. She felt Race tense, his free hand grasping the back of her neck, tangling in her hair, and desperation made her bolder; she had come too far to back down now, and his body wasn't entirely indifferent to her caress, she let her tongue explore the vulnerable area discovered by her lips, feeling the explosive reaction of the taut skin, closing her mouth over it experimentally, and hearing Race groan hoarsely, his fingers buried in her hair as he tried to lift her head.

'Heather, for God's sake,' she heard him mutter thickly when he couldn't move her, and her fingers moved teasingly over his stomach, lower and lower until he moaned harshly. 'Heather, for God's sake stop. If you don't, you could well find yourself in exactly the same position again. Surely you don't want another child—of mine. . . .'

'And if I do?' She raised her head, to look at him, stunned by the pain and raw aching she saw in his eyes, her fingers stilling as she watched him.

'Heather!' He groaned her name protestingly, and something warm and sweet seemed to melt inside her, her voice a soft sigh of pleasure as she lay down beside him, twining her arms round his neck. He did want her!

She covered his face with small kisses, teasing the taut line of his mouth with her tongue, revelling in his harsh moan of protest as his hands claimed her breasts, his mouth buried in the warm curve of her throat. 'Heather . . . you shouldn't do this,' he said thickly. 'God knows I don't want to hurt you . . . but, darling, I've wanted this for so long. . . .'

Darling, he had called her darling! Heather's heart sang, giving her the confidence to push aside the bedclothes and entwine him with her body, immediately feeling his searing, heated response. His mouth and hands devoured her hungrily, making her gasp in fierce arousal as his tongue explored the moist cavity of her mouth, his the initiative now as his hands moved strokingly over her body. 'Oh God,' he moaned into her skin, 'I want to touch and taste every inch of you. . . . You don't know what you do to me. . . .'

'Show me.' She whispered it against his ear, watching his eyes darken in disbelief, suddenly mischievously happy, as she let her fingers drift over the hard angle of his hip, and felt the surge of need he couldn't hide as he cried her name harshly and moved against her, his lips gentle against her breast, the darkness of his head against her unleashing the same tenderness she experienced with Robert.

'Heather, why are you doing this?' She went still as she heard the tortured huskiness of his voice. 'You must know how hard I've tried not to let this happen; staying in London, keeping away from you until my body aches with the pain of wanting you. I thought I could make you love me. . . . I willed you to love me,' he told her, his eyes dark with pain.

'From the first moment I saw your photograph I wanted you. I was obsessed by you,' he admitted, letting his lips linger over the satin skin of her shoulder. 'I found out about Jennifer and persuaded Terry to introduce you to me, only it didn't work; you rejected me, but I still wanted you—so badly that I think I went a little mad. I'd heard about your reputation with other men and couldn't understand why you wanted them but you didn't want me. That was when I planned to trap you at the cottage. I thought if I got you alone . . . I *wanted* to make you pregnant,' he admitted, astounding her, his lips unable to resist the tormenting appeal of her peaked nipple, a sweetly aching pain piercing Heather as she caught the small sound of satisfaction moving his throat as he gave in to the temptation. Her fingers stroked gently through his hair as she tried to absorb what he had said.

'I thought if I did you would have to marry me,' he added, reluctantly releasing her warm flesh. 'I didn't want to be like all the others—allowed to share your bed for a while and then discarded. I wanted you too much for that. And then I found out you were a virgin.'

He shook his head as though the discovery still pained him. 'I wanted to kill myself,' he admitted unevenly. 'I couldn't understand how I'd been crass enough not to see it for myself. . . . My only justification was that I was so fathoms deep in love with you that I couldn't see anything but that. . . .'

'You *loved* me?'

'Love, in the present tense . . . Did love, do love, will love. . . .' Race murmured softly, punctuating the words with tender kisses.

'But you were so angry. . . . You wanted me to leave the cottage. . . .'

'Because I couldn't live with what I'd done,' Race groaned. 'Can't you understand that? I told myself it was only fair to let you go, but that didn't stop me trying to tear London apart to find you. Jen wouldn't tell me where you'd gone. God, when I saw that damned newspaper, I thought I was hallucinating. I couldn't believe it. . . . I couldn't rest until I knew. I found out Neil's address, I went to find him and saw your aunt and uncle. Your aunt guessed immediately who I was. . . . Between us we fixed it so that I could see you. Once I knew the baby was mine I was determined not to let you go.'

'Then all those things you told me. . . .'

'Were true,' he told her firmly, 'but more important than any of them was the fact that I loved you. I was so jealous of Neil, and still am. I thought tonight you were just relieving your frustration of wanting him, and then when you said you wanted. . . .'

'To have your baby?' Heather whispered, smiling. 'And I meant it, Race,' she murmured against his throat, seeking and finding the sensitive core of maleness and stroking it with her tongue, until he pushed her away from him, 'but this time, I'd prefer if we didn't succeed first time,' she said demurely.

Oh God, if she hadn't come to him tonight, how long would they have gone on in mutual misery?

As though he had read her thoughts, Race said huskily, 'I couldn't have endured much more. When I came home today and saw you with the baby. . . .'

He closed his eyes, and Heather saw the dampness clinging to his lashes. 'God, I was so jealous, of my own child. And when you were having him. . . . They told me that you kept calling for me. I couldn't believe it. I felt so helpless watching you struggle, I wanted to bear the pain for you, but instead what I had done was cause it. I've never been so terrified by anything in my whole life!'

'It takes two, you know,' Heather reminded him, nuzzling his shoulder and feeling his arm tighten round her. 'We've both been blind, Race. I know with hindsight that I was attracted to you from the first; I think I fell in love with you the first time I saw you, but we weren't looking properly at one another, we were just seeing images of what we'd expected to see. I was jealous too,' she admitted, 'of Davinia Fane.'

'*Davinia?*' The open incredulity in his voice warmed her heart.

'You were mentioned together in the gossip columns. I thought you were staying in London to be near her.'

'When in reality I was staying there because I knew it was the only way I could keep my hands off you. When you came to me tonight. . . . why did you. . . .?' His hands were exploring the supple shape of her body, reason abandoned to desire as she moved sensuously against their warmth.

'Because I thought you'd come down to tell me you wanted a divorce, and I wanted you so badly.'

'How badly?' he drawled, with an unanticipated resurgence of his former control.

'Very badly,' Heather admitted huskily. 'These last few months I've thought I hallucinated you making love to me; that I'd just imagined it all.'

'Umm ... tell me,' Race murmured against her skin, 'Was this how you imagined it ... and this...?' His heart thudded against her, his body hardening against her as she responded feverishly to his lovemaking, the love-words and pleas his voice murmured against her skin echoing the rhythm of their bodies.

'Race ... oh ... oh, Race,' she protested feebly, only partially satisfied by the warm stroke of his hand along her inner thigh, her body welcoming and recognising the tense breath he exhaled as his control splintered and his hands slid under her thighs, lifting her towards him. 'Heather, I don't want to hurt you,' he protested when she arched her body into his, rejoicing in the thrusting arousal he was fighting to control. 'When Robert was born. . . .'

'The only way you can hurt me, Race Williams,' she whispered lovingly against his ear, her fingers finding and smoothing lovingly the muscles of his back, 'is by not loving me. I want you, Race,' she said quietly, 'I desire you, I need you, I love you.'

Her fingernails raked over his back as he moved against her and into her, her small gasp of pleasure silenced by his lips, her body rising joyously to meet the demand of his. . . .

It was some time later when the sound of Robert crying broke her deeply peaceful sleep. She had gone to sleep in Race's arms, enfolded by his body, still enraptured by the pleasure they had shared; the knowledge that he loved her. But now Race was gone. Opening her eyes, she struggled to sit up, her eyes widening as she saw Race perched on the end of the bed, Robert in his arms.

'He was crying,' he told her softly, 'I think he's probably hungry.'

'I'm sure of it,' Heather agreed, glancing at her watch. 'But it won't hurt him to go a little hungry for once,' she added cheerfully. 'After all, sooner or later he's going to discover that he's only the second most important male in my life.'

She was rewarded with a smile that dissolved the last of her doubts. 'I'm hungry too,' Race told her. 'I'll go down and make us something to eat while you feed him. I was too wrought up to eat before. I told myself I'd stay away this weekend, I wouldn't torment myself by coming down to see you knowing you didn't want me, but somehow I found myself in my car driving down here. I half expected to find Neil with you.'

'Neil's perfectly happy with Sue,' Heather told him softly. 'He always knew that I loved you.'

'When I saw that blasted pram I nearly wanted to commit murder,' Race admitted wryly, 'but that was nothing compared to how I felt when I discovered that he had been the one to drive you to the hospital. He. . . .'

'But you were the one I wanted,' Heather interrupted. 'I love Neil as a brother, but it was you, my lover, my husband, the father of my child, that I wanted with me——'

'I'd better go down and fix us something to eat,' Race told her, 'otherwise our son might find himself going without another meal.' His eyes were tender as he handed Robert over to her, plumping up the pillows behind her so that she could lean back, watching in fascination for a few seconds as Robert started to suck, and then bending his head to kiss her gently.

He paused at the door and turned. 'I love you, Heather,' he said softly, and she knew it was true. She could see his love in his eyes, feel it, filling the room, almost tangibly so. 'Don't spend too long in the kitchen, then,' she said demurely, 'so that you can show me.'

The look in his eyes reminded her of the way he had looked at her when she first saw him, and her body responded to it immediately. It took Robert's protesting yell to remind his parents of his existence, and as she heard Race walk downstairs smiled dreamily down at her son.

'He loves me,' she whispered, as Robert stared back at her uncomprehendingly, 'and I love him ... and you, my little love, could very soon find yourself exiled to the nursery!'

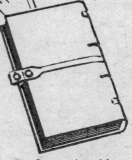

Take these 4 best-selling novels FREE

Harlequin Photo ~ Calendar ~

Turn Your Favorite Photo into a Calendar.

JULY 1984

The Browns

Uniquely yours, this 10x17½" calendar features your favorite photograph, with any name you wish in attractive lettering at the bottom. A delightfully personal and practical idea!

Send us your favorite color print, black-and-white print, negative, or slide, any size (we'll return it), along with **3** proofs of purchase (coupon below) from a June or July release of Harlequin Romance, Harlequin Presents, Harlequin Superromance, Harlequin American Romance or Harlequin Temptation, plus $5.75 (includes shipping and handling).

Harlequin Photo Calendar Offer
(PROOF OF PURCHASE)

NAME_____
(Please Print)

ADDRESS_____

CITY_____ STATE_____ ZIP_____

NAME ON CALENDAR_____

Mail photo, 3 proofs,   **Harlequin Books**   2-6
plus check or money order   P.O. Box 52020
for $5.75 payable to: Phoenix, AZ 85072

Offer expires December 31, 1984. (Not available in Canada)   CAL-1